"This book will be prized by teachers, authors, students, and all readers who value the use of folklore, mythology, and the familiar stories of youth. A pleasure to read; highly recommended."
—*Library Journal*

"Thought-provoking perspectives on reading and appreciating fantasy."
—*Booklist*

"Each essay inspires and awakens the creative spirit, and each is worth reading again and again."
—*Rambles*

"Should be required reading for teachers, librarians, and parents especially."
—*Children's Book Review Service*

JANE YOLEN

TOUCH MAGIC

Fantasy, Faerie & Folklore
in the Literature of Childhood

EXPANDED EDITION

August House Publishers, Inc.
LITTLE ROCK

10 9 8 7 6 5 4 3 2

Library of Congress Cataloging in Publication Data
Yolen, Jane.
    Touch magic : fantasy, faerie & folklore in the literature of childhood /
Jane Yolen.—
    Expanded ed.
        p.   cm.
        "Books for further reading"—p.
    ISBN 0-87483-591-7 (pbk. : acid-free paper)
    1. Folklore and children. 2. Children's stories—Psychological aspects.
3. Fantasy in children. I. Title.

GR43.C4 Y64 2000
398'.083—dc21   00-027565

ACKNOWLEDGMENTS

Portions of these essays, in slightly altered forms, have appeared in the following magazines: *Horn Book, Parents' Choice, Children's Literature in Education,
Language Arts, The Writer, Childhood Education, CMLEA Journal, Top of the
News, In Touch, Parabola, Massachusetts Primer,* and in the column "Bookfare"
in *The Daily Hampshire Gazette.*

The story entitled "Story, the old man said," on page 120 is ©1993 by Jane Yolen.

Interior illustrations from the designs of Wilhelm von Kaulbach.
Cover art by Don Bell; cover design by Joy Freeman.
Cover photo by Jason Stemple, ©2000.
August House editorial team: Joy Freeman, Jody McNeese.

AUGUST HOUSE PUBLISHERS, INC.

For the great magic makers of the past,
the storytellers,
who have reminded us of our humanity.

Contents

To My Readers:

This book of essays was written because I believe that culture begins in the cradle. Literature is a continuous process from childhood onward, not a body of work sprung full-blown from the heads of adults who never read or were read to as children. Further, I believe that the continuum of literature is best maintained by those tales of fantasy, fancy, faerie, and the supra-natural, those crafted visions and bits and pieces of dream-remembering that link our past and our future. To do without tales and stories and books is to lose humanity's past, is to have no star map for our future.

But a story has to have two equal partners, tale teller and tale listener. And so these essays, from a storyteller to an audience: listen, touch magic, and pass it on.

Jane Yolen, Phoenix Farm
Hatfield, Massachusetts
1981

A New Edition:

When *Touch Magic* was first published by Philomel Books in 1981, a slim volume of essays about fantasy, faerie, and folklore in the literature of childhood, it was greeted with huzzahs. Professors assigned it as reading in folklore, storytelling, and early education classes.

But other readers took to the book, too. I have found quotes from the book (especially "Touch magic—pass it on...") on internet web sites, in PhD theses, and on AOL members' profiles.

When the book went out of print, about five years ago, I began to get letters from desperate teachers, readers, fans begging for copies.

So here—with thanks to the wonderful folks at August House— is *Touch Magic* once again. This time around there is an additional section with six new essays in which I talk about the early touchstones of children's fantasy, puzzle over problems of time travel, try to come up with a definition of story, explore the problems of fantasy authors being mired in society, and take a fresh look at the morality of fairy tales.

So—touch magic once again, and pass it on.

Jane Yolen, Wayside
St. Andrews, Scotland
1999

PART ONE
The Tale and the Teller

How Basic Is Shazam?

If one were preparing a slide show to represent children in a myth-less age, it might go something like this:

CLICK. A hundred thousand boys and girls in front of their TV sets shouting "Shazam!"

CLICK. An advertisement in a serious teachers' magazine for "Phonics Comix" with a picture of Spider-Man on the top.

CLICK. Teenagers whose knowledge of the gods of ancient Greece, Rome, and the classical age is bounded by Xena on one side and Hercules on the other.

CLICK. A classroom full of children watching a movie about Apollo—the space program.

CLICK. A class of freshmen at Boston College taking an identification test, measuring their ability to recall names from the great religions and mythologies of the past. Well over half miss the name "King David."

CLICK. A class at the prestigious women's college, Smith, listening to a paper on Keats's "La Belle Dame Sans Merci." Asking for a reference explanation, one senior asks, "Did you make up that Lilith?"

No. Nor would these pictures be "made up" either. They and hundreds of others just as telling are part of a growing body of anecdotes that point to the fact that we are well on the way to the de-mythologizing of our human existence. Our children are growing up without their birthright: the myths, fairy tales, fantasies, and folklore that are their proper legacy. It is a serious loss.

Who was Lilith? King David? Pegasus? Anansi the Spider? Apollo? Or the six whose names originally formed the acronym SHAZAM in the "Captain Marvel" spell: Solomon, Hercules, Atlas, Zeus, Achilles, Mercury?

In fact, *Shazam* itself has become a mnemonic for instant change and nothing more; this transformation is perhaps the deepest, sharpest metaphor for what is happening to our children today.

* * *

Mythology, legend, the lore of the folk, those tales that were once as real to their believers as a sunrise, hardly exist today even as reference points. In our haste to update educational standards, we have done away with the older gods, so that now all that we have left are names without faces, mnemonics without meaning.

Over the last few years there have been many educational councils and conferences, papers and presentations about the need to return to the Basics—to the teaching of the fundamental skills of reading, writing and arithmetic. But they are not the only subjects that are vital to our intellectual and human growth. An understanding of, a grounding in, a familiarity with the old lores and wisdoms of the so-called dead worlds is also a basic developmental need. Folklorist Charles Potter has written that "Folklore is a lively fossil that refuses to die." If children are invited to meet the great stories, to shake hands with the lively fossil, they will soon discover—as did their parents before them—that the well-kept bones are indispensable to the life of the mind. Myth and legend and folklore can serve

14

four very basic functions in the education of Everychild.

One of the basic functions of myth and folk literature is to provide a landscape of allusion. With the first story a child hears, he or she takes a step toward perceiving a new environment, one that is filled with quests and questers, fated heroes and fetid monsters, intrepid heroines and trepid helpers, even incompetent oafs who achieve competence and wholeness by going out and trying. As the child hears more stories and tales that are linked in both obvious and subtle ways, that landscape is broadened and deepened, and becomes more fully populated with memorable characters. These are the same folk that the child will meet again and again, threading their archetypal ways throughout the cultural history of our planet.

Stories lean on stories, art on art. This familiarity with the treasure-house of ancient story is necessary for any true appreciation of today's literature. A child who has never met Merlin—how can he or she really recognize the wizards in Earthsea? The child who has never heard of Arthur—how can he or she totally appreciate Susan Cooper's *The Grey King*? The child who has never known dryads or fauns will not recognize them in Narnia, or find their faces on museum walls or in the black silhouettes on Greek vases. Never to have trod the stony paths of Mount Pelion with Chiron and to have seen only the sexually precocious centaurs of *Fantasia* or the horsemen on TV's *Hercules* is to be diminished, narrowed, condemned to live in a cultural landscape that is dry as dust.

The second function of folklore is to provide a way of looking at another culture from the inside out. If a child becomes familiar with the pantheon of Greek gods, who toy with human lives as carelessly as children at play, then the Greek world view begins to come into focus. If a child learns about the range of Norse godlings who wait for heroic companions to feast with them at Valhalla, then the Vikings' emphasis on battle derring-do makes more sense. The study of the myth-making process, of those things that come together in a culture and propel a folk towards a coherent mythology, may be a very sophisticated one indeed, but its beginnings are back in the tales themselves.

Stories lean on stories, cultures on cultures. Just as any great city is built upon the bones and stones of its ancestors, so too is any mythology. And if our children can look at their own modern folk-lore within a broader context, they will see some very surprising shadows indeed. Spider-Man and TV's Hercules, Buffy and Xena do not spring from a void but from needs within our own culture. And those needs lean on past needs.

Maureen Duffy writes in *The Erotic World of Faery:*

> We remake our mythology in every age out of our own needs. We may use ideas lying around loose from a previous system or systems as part of the fabric. The human situation doesn't radically alter and therefore certain myths are constantly reappearing.

Thus, for example, in the adaptable Spider-Man who helps the poor, the vulnerable, and the helpless we see Prometheus and Robin Hood, though his abilities also echo the African Anansi the Spider. In the compassion and strength of Hercules we see Atlas and Samson and Paul Bunyan. Xena and Buffy both spring directly from Diana the Huntress and the Amazons, propelled by the electronic revolution and feminist rage.

This is mythic archeology, probing now for then, splitting the present to find the past. It works because humans have always had, in folklorist Joseph Campbell's fine phrase, "a long backward reach."

***

Providing a landscape of allusion and a knowledge of ancestral cultures are the two most obvious functions of mythology in the intellectual development of the child. But the next two functions are more complex and also more important.

According to Albert Lavin, "Myth conceived of as symbolic form...[is] a way of organizing the human response to reality...[and is] a fundamental aspect of the way we 'process' experience." By extension, in Lavin's view and also in the view of Dr. Bruno Bettelheim, the noted child psychologist whose book *The Uses of Enchantment* exploded onto the literary scene in 1976, myth becomes a marvelously adaptable tool of therapy.

Like a kaleidoscope, a folktale is made up of large and small units—motifs—incidents that, like bits of colored glass, are picked up as the tale travels from story to story, from country to country, from culture to culture. Shake up the folktale kaleidoscope, and these motifs rearrange themselves in an infinite variety of usable and attractive forms. Stith Thompson's monumental *Motif Index of Folk Literature* gives a view of the range of these forms. If the therapists need an archetypal evil stepmother or wicked natural mother, they can simply shake the folkloroscope and find one in a variant of a Cinderella story or a Medea myth. If a heroic conquest of a giant parent-figure is called for, they can shake and take Jack and his beanstalk or the story of Polyphemus or Beowulf. If the problem centers around a downtrodden, seemingly simpleton son, they can use the Fool-of-the-World story or any of its variations.

The idea of folklore as a tool for psychotherapy found its best articulation in Bettelheim's book, in which he wrote: "The fairy tale is a verification of the interior life of the child." The emphasis, in this case, is on immediate *applicability,* on the *use* of the archetypes in these stories to mold a mentally stable individual.

The fourth function of myth and fantasy, while related to this one, is much subtler and much more important. The great archetypal stories provide a framework or model for an individual's belief system. They are, in Isak Dinesen's marvelous expression, "a serious statement of our existence." The tales and stories handed down to us from the cultures that preceded us were the most serious, succinct expressions of the accumulated wisdom of those cultures. They were created in a symbolic, metaphoric story language and then honed by centuries of tongue-polishing to a crystalline perfection.

Symbolic language is something that a young child seems to understand almost viscerally; metaphoric speech is the child's own speech, though it is without analytic thought: a black cat is called "Midnight," a white dog named "Snowball"—immediate metaphors. Thus even very young children can absorb the meanings and wisdom of these symbolically expressed ancient tales and use them as tools for interpreting their own day-to-day experiences.

Myth as serious statement plays an important role in the life of the child. It can be the child's key to understanding his or her own existence. It can also be the key to our understanding of the child. William Butler Yeats has written, "There is some one myth for every man which, if we but knew it, would make us understand all he did and thought."

These four functions of myth and folklore should establish the listening to and learning of the old tales as being among the most basic elements of our education: creating a landscape of allusion, enabling us to understand our own and other cultures from the inside out, providing an adaptable tool of therapy, and stating in symbolic or metaphoric terms the abstract truths of our common human existence.

And if we deny our children their cultural, historical heritage, their birthright to these stories, what then? Instead of creating men and women who have a grasp of literary allusion and symbolic language, and a metaphorical tool for dealing with the serious problems of life, we will be forming stunted boys and girls who speak only a barren language, a language that accurately reflects their equally barren minds. Language helps develop life as surely as it reflects life. It is a most important part of our human condition.

Our children today face a serious deprivation—the loss of the word, of words. For as stories depend on stories, lives depend on lives. Contact and continuity are essential links in the long chain of human culture. One should not be seduced by the idea of the noble savage. The feral child deprived of all human contact does not become a Mowgli or a Tarzan, conversant with the animals. Lacking human language, he lacks true memory and thus lacks the ability to learn. Without mythology or art he cannot generalize or interpret his experience. Running on four limbs, he is slower than the beasts he follows, less agile than the humans he flees. His lifespan is diminished, his mental span likewise. In reality, the feral child does not live as a god in the jungle, but as a being rather less than human and not as well adapted as a beast.

We are in danger of creating our own feral children when we deny them access to their inheritance of story. When we let them run free with only their minimal animal demands on language, or deprive them of the insights and poetic visions expressed in words that humans have produced throughout human history, we deny them—in the end—their own humanity.

A child conversant with the old tales accepts them with an ease born of familiarity, fitting them into his own scheme of things, endowing them with new meaning. That old fossil, those old bones, walk again, and sing and dance and speak with a new tongue. The old stories bridge the centuries.

The Lively Fossil

In earlier days the storyteller knew the backgrounds of his audience intimately, knew their limits, their desires, their demands, their fears. But storytellers today no longer live in a small village. We live in what, for want of a better term, we call a global village. The modern storyteller knows that the printed tale speaks to an audience many thousands of miles wide.

Where once storytellers carried traditions on their tongues, letting those gems drop before their listeners with the ease of the girl with her mouth full of diamonds, today's storytellers are eclectic. A writer of stories today may, for example, know not only the *dybbuks* and *golems* of Eastern Europe, but the selchies of Orkney and Shetland, the gorgons of Greece, Baba Yaga and her chicken-footed hut, and the Aztec Caotlicue and her ball of feathers; they may use Loki the trickster of the North as readily as Africa's Trickster Hare. The old stories had a habit of changing as they passed from one tongue to another, kept alive by a sort of mouth-to-mouth resuscitation. Listeners sometimes resisted changes in a story they knew and loved—and yet, think how changed that story must already have been, from its misty origins to the contemporary rendition.

From mouth to ear to mouth, the old tales went. It was a generational art, a regenerational art, passed on and on. Each story was a cultural heirloom, preserving traditions in strange and sometimes original ways. Cinderella, arising somewhere in preliterate China, brought along vestiges of footbinding with its emphasis on the tiny shoe. The briar in Sleeping Beauty encapsulated the Druidic language of trees, which sees the briar as signifying eroticism.

These stories underwent continuous change, for they were not carved in stone, not yet set in wood or metal type to repeat themselves endlessly and perfectly on the white page. Instead they were reshaped with each telling by one of three tellers: the blind beggar, the nursery maid, or the clerk. So the great ballad collector, Francis James Child, who collected all the "Child ballads," named them.

The "blind beggar," of course, is the street-corner storyteller, telling his tales for a penny or two. If the audience likes what it hears, he makes enough to buy himself bread and wine and a pallet for the night. If not...well, he has gone hungry before. But he prefers to eat, and this preference for food forces him to change his stories to suit his listeners.

The "nursery maid" tells stories to her charges, the young masters and mistresses. She wants them to grow up with a sense of morality—and she does not want them to have nightmares when she puts them in their beds to sleep at night. So she changes the tales she tells them to make her own particular points.

And the "clerk" is the writer or recorder who serves only the word of the tale; the poet or singer who changes the tales to suit his audience of one, the self.

Thus the oldest stories were transmitted and transmuted, the kaleidoscope patterns of motif changed by time and by the times, by the tellers and by the listeners, by the country in which they arose and the countries to which they were carried. The old oral tales were changed the way culture itself changes, the way traditions change, by an erosion/eruption as powerful in its way as any geological force.

Follow a story through its variants and you are following the trade routes, the slave routes, the route of a conquering army, or that of a restless people on the move.

If the oral tradition came first, the second type of tale came hard on its heels. Once writing was established, the written word worked its own magic on the world of story. Even before the invention of movable type, which was the fifteenth century's greatest contribution to culture, the transcribed story had been part of the story process.

But when an oral tale was set down, something interesting happened. The particular variant rendered into writing took on borrowed authority from the page. Quite simply, it *became* the tale. Not only listeners seated in a particular audience at a particular time could hear the tale. Audiences separated by time and space could hear it as well.

Authority is a word that grew from the root *author*. And so author and power became inextricably linked. By setting down a tale onto a page, the scribe became the "owner" of a story. And if a particular reteller had wit, style, and a large printing, he had an incredible impact on the tale.

Take Charles Perrault, a seventeenth-century French civil servant who collected and rewrote a group of popular stories which he published in 1697 (the book later appeared in England under the title *Mother Goose Tales*). One of the stories was "Cendrillon." It was a Cinderella variant and, though the Ash-girl had been around Europe and the Orient in one form or another for centuries, Perrault added a fairy godmother, a midnight warning and—by an accident of bad translation—a glass slipper. (*De vair* means "of fur, ermine, or variegated fur"; *de verre* means "of glass.") Perrault changed the Cinderella story for all time. When most children and adults are asked to tell the story, those three elements are nearly always included in their recitals. Such is the power of print. What is written becomes the accepted standard. In fact, not until 1950, when the Walt Disney *Cinderella* was released, did the story receive another such noticeable change.

The transcribed tale, then, is midway between the oral, from which it springs, and the literary fairy tale, to which it points. It is a conscious reshaping of old materials, but stays within the limits of the traditional story. Yet when a brilliant transcriber such as Perrault (or Madame Leprince de Beaumont, who wrote "Beauty and the Beast" in its best-remembered form) writes a story, it becomes his or her tale for all time.

23

The third type of folk story is not from folk at all. It is the eclectic literary or art tale. Many different sources are pulled together as the author composes it. The art tale is modern and ancient at once and it remains essentially in the written form because it was born that way.

So Hans Christian Andersen draws on his lower-class background and the many stories he heard as a child, crosses them with his longing to be handsome and to be accepted in Danish society, and writes "The Ugly Duckling." Or he immortalizes in "The Emperor's Nightingale" his love for Jenny Lind, the Swedish Nightingale whose pure voice meant more to him than the artifices of the divas of the Royal Opera.

There are people today writing this kind of tale. First of all, as any storyteller knows, the art tale must tell a good story. Storytelling may be the oldest of all the arts: the mother told a story to her child, the hunter to his peers, the survivor to his rescuers, the priestess to her followers, the seer to his petitioners. They did not just report facts, *they told a tale.* And the better the tale was told, the more it was believed. And the more it was believed, the truer it became. (Isaac Bashevis Singer, a master storyteller himself, has said: "In art, truth that is boring is not true.") The best of the old stories spoke to the listener because they spoke not just to the ears but to the heart as well.

And what is a story? Something with a beginning, a middle, and an end, of course. But the lasting stories are more. If they are lacking that bit of "inner truth," if they do not make Dinesen's "serious statement," then they are of no value. Without meaning, without metaphor, without reaching out to touch human emotion, a story is a poor thing: a few rags upon a stick masquerading as a living creature. Storytelling is our oldest form of remembering the promises we have made to one another and to our various gods, and the promises given in return; it is a way of recording our human emotions and desires and taboos. Whoever dares to tell a story must bear in mind that the story is an essential part of our humanness. But of course it had better be an engrossing, well-told tale as well.

Further, the best new stories have something serious to say about the writer and his or her particular world. All writers write about themselves, just as the old storytellers chose to tell stories that spoke to and about themselves. They call it the world, but it is themselves they portray. The world of which they write is like a mirror that reflects the inside of their hearts, often more truly than they know.

So the writer writes about himself or herself when writing an art tale, and tries to make a serious statement within the confines of an absorbing tale. But he or she writes in a sort of code, a symbolic language. That code can be read on many levels. The child reads it on one, the adult on another. The artist reads it differently from the analyst. My husband reads it differently from my sons. And I read it another way still.

In the same way, we hear different "readings" of an old tale. Take "Little Red Riding Hood." Anthropologists have read it as a folk memory of old menstruation myths or sun/moon myths. Freudians point to it as a possible incest story, or a pregnancy fantasy. Marxists have seen it as the triumph of the proletariat over the evil capitalists who would lure them into a cozy relationship and then devour them. And moralists through the ages say it means simply: Young women should not go to bed with strangers who may turn out to be "wolves." Who is right? They are *all* right. For as the writer writes about himself or herself solipsistically, so the adult reader reads.

But a child, more open than the adult, is more changed by that reading. Just as the child is born with a literal hole in its head, where the bones slowly close underneath the fragile shield of skin, so the child is born with a figurative hole in its heart. Slowly this, too, is filled up. What slips in before it anneals shapes the man or woman into which that child will grow. Story is one of the most serious intruders into the heart.

The creators of modern literary tales for the young must recognize this, deep down, when they write. The child reading the fairy tale takes it—and the writer (for the story *is* the writer)—into his heart. There is a literary Eucharist: heart to heart, body to body, blood to blood. The writer is parent to all children who read what he or she writes.

***

25

Such stories—oral tales and transcribed tales and literary folk tales—have had their detractors. From time immemorial, all kinds of people have railed against them. They "injure the tender minds of children by exciting unreasonable and groundless fears," ran one school of thought expressed by English children's book author Mrs. Sarah Trimmer in the early 1800s. "Cinderella" has been called a story encouraging shoe-fetishism, and "Beauty and the Beast" a thinly veiled paean to bestial sex. It sometimes seems that the more ludicrous the charge, the more likely it is to be believed.

What are these stories that they excite such passions on either side? And why, in a world in which people can fly in a metal box faster than Pegasus could even gain the sky, should we still read and write them? Because, as Charles Potter tells us, these stories are part of a lively fossil that refuses to die. Because they speak to the human condition.

The German poet Johann Schiller said it plainly: "Deeper meaning resides in the fairy tales told me in my childhood than in any truth that is taught in life." And G. K. Chesterton wrote: "If you really read the fairy tales, you will observe that one idea runs from one end of them to the other—the idea that peace and happiness can only exist on some condition. This idea, which is the core of ethics, is the core of the nursery tale."

***

Folklore reflects the society that creates it. Modern art tales, borrowing characters and cadences from the folk, take on this mirroring quality, too. They reflect both the individual and the society. It would be naive to think otherwise.

But these stories come out of and then go back into society, changing the shape of that society in turn. The old tales were part of the belief system of the class of people who listened to and learned from and believed in them, the folk who, in William Butler Yeats's wonderful phrase, "steeped everything in the heart." Children today are that class. And so the modern mythmakers, knowing how powerful the tales can be, must not, like the old gods, bear this burden lightly.

Once Upon a Time

Anyone who has watched children growing up and observed the magic of their transformations cannot help but be amazed by the process. It is an expected and yet unexpected series of changes that are almost imperceptible on a day-to-day basis. Yet they relentlessly evolve from microscopic dots to tadpoles to bug-eyed fetuses to naked squalling infants to mischief-bent toddlers to dirt-smudged schoolchildren to adolescents at the mercy of hormonal dreams. It is hard even for a mother to identify the toddler and the teenager as the same child or chart the changes wrought in a short fourteen years by time, by society, by the physical demands of life. Much of it must be taken on faith.

In the same way, we follow the changeling life of a fairy tale across centuries. It can only be done by a kind of faith in the integrity of the story and a few signposts. Just as one can check out the whorls of an adult's thumbprints against those infant-small prints that were pressed onto a page soon after birth, so one can find similar prints on the body of any tale. They are the thumbprints of history, but they are harder to read than any yellowing birth certificate or a well-loved photograph in a family album.

* * *

The tale of Little Red Riding Hood, for example, bears such prints, smudged but still readable. Despite the fact that Charles Dickens once claimed that Little Red Riding Hood was his first true love and that marriage to her would have meant he "should have known perfect bliss," there are many ambivalences about the tale.

Does it end with the snap of the wolf's jaws? Does it end with the woodcutter passing by as conveniently as the mounted troopers in old Westerns, his sharp axe at the ready? Or should it end like the Grimms' story number five, "The Wolf and the Seven Young Kids," in which the wolf is punished with a bellyful of stones and death by drowning?

A first-grade teacher in a private laboratory school attached to a major women's college conducted an interesting experiment in this regard. She was a children's book fan and a believer in the efficacy of storytelling. Brave soul, she taught the children about storytelling and variants, and concluded by reading them three different versions of the Red Riding Hood tale. This happened near the end of the Vietnam War, and the children came from academic families in which the parents were prone to discussing the horrors of war at the table and inviting the children to watch the instant replay of destruction on the television set as part of their education.

The teacher asked the children in her class to vote for their own favorite ending to Red Riding Hood: wolf feast, woodcutter-take-all, or the stone stomach-ache with a trip downriver.

Much to the surprise of every adult (although it would not have surprised William Golding, who charted childhood's thirst for cruel justice in *Lord of the Flies*), the children opted for ending number three because it made the wolf suffer more. It was a long, drawn-out, nasty ending but quite tidy, even to the neat disposal of the corpse.

But if endings differ according to the morality of teller and listener, the bones of the story have not changed. Scholars point to a thirteenth-century version of the famous story in the *Elder Edda*. Thor is disguised as the bride of a giant he wishes to slay. Loki must explain to the nervous bridegroom why his bride looks so strange:

"Why are Freya's eyes so ghastly?" asks the giant Thrym, catching a glimpse of them under the veil.

"Because she has such a longing to see you," says Loki. "She has had no sleep for eight nights."

And in an early French version of Red Riding Hood, as recounted by W. H. Auden in *The Dyer's Hand,* the wolf invites the little girl to "undress, my child, and come and sleep beside me." There follows a detailed disrobing as the child discards apron, bodice, dress, skirt, hose. Into the fire they must go because, as the wolf admonishes her, "you will need them no more."

And then the now-familiar ritual begins. But how different it sounds to an adult's ears:

O Grandmother, how hairy you are.
 It's to keep me warmer my child.
O Grandmother, those long nails you have.
 It's to scratch me better my child.
O Grandmother those big shoulders you have.
 All the better to carry kindling from the woods, my child.
O Grandmother, what big ears you have.
 All the better to hear with my child.
O Grandmother, the big mouth you have.
 All the better to eat you with my child.
O Grandmother, I need to go outside to relieve myself.
 Do it in the bed, my child.

At this point, the child realizes her mistake. That is not something that Grandmother would have said. There is more here than frilly nightgown, a lace-ribboned cap, and a hairy snout. Something else, something sinister, is lurking under the bedclothes. The child begs to go outside and finally, with a string tied around her leg to keep her chained to the false grandmother, she leaves. Once outside, she manages to untie the knot and run off home.

But it is still the same tale, though a variety of clean-minded nursery maid tellers have gotten their hands on it somewhere along the way.

There are very few wolves left in the world, a tragedy with ecological repercussions. But there are many wolves still left under the bedclothes, and that is why the tale still lives.

***

J. R. R. Tolkien has written: "If men really could not distinguish between frogs and men, fairy stories about frogkings would not have arisen." In the beginning, of course, there really was little distinguishing between frogs and men. That is, a totemistic tribe that worshiped a frog considered frogs as friends, ancestors, saviors, and infinitely more like themselves than any one of the human tribe of wolf-worshipers living down the road. So, too, a child relates easily to his pet goldfish, his kitten, and his stuffed bear while ignoring the new neighbor or an elderly aunt.

Allegory is a development of that childlike belief, for as the child and the race grow up, so does the ability to distinguish between frogs and men. That small, green, glistening ounce of hop over there is a frog. That tall, hairy, striding hulk over there is a prince. Even if each is wearing a crown, they are distinguishable.

But the growing intelligence says more. It says: There is something of frog in every prince and conversely something of prince in every frog. And so the frog-prince story arises.

It has been traced back through the Grimms' version to earlier German household tales; it has been traced even further in its English variants, to a sixteenth-century collection of story titles found amongst Scottish shepherds. And Sir Walter Scott, that often fanciful folklorist, who made up things when he couldn't find proper sources for them (or as he wrote: "I could never repeat a story without giving it a new hat and stick"), thought the frog was related to tales of crocodiles told by the Kalmuck Tartars. There has even been unsubstantiated argument that our friend the frog-prince is related to the famous Green Knight whom Gawain beheads but does not kill.

It is a transformation tale, one of a great line of shapeshifting stories that fill the world's fairy tale coffers. It contains this bit of wisdom: that a princely person might be contained in a loathsome skin. That familiar theme has been played on folk instruments, orchestrated in ballads such as "Allison Gross," myths such as "Cupid and Psyche," and tales such as Madame Leprince de Beaumont's "Beauty and the Beast." And of course, it also lies at the heart of psychotherapy.

But the theme is buried in the tale, the golden yolk inside the egg of story. So the German storyteller starts "In olden times, when wishing still helped…" And, more direct, the English version begins "One fine evening a young princess went into a wood…"

And there she meets a frog, a most persuasive speaker, nicer and even more humane than the princess herself. He, after all, keeps his end of a bargain made at the wellspring, the source of life for the frog. What he asks is not considered forward, since he is a frog.

Later on, the German and English versions fudge a bit about what happens in the princess's bedroom, skipping from night to morning in a single sentence. That is how it should be. This is a frog, after all, not a prince, who is locked up all night in her boudoir.

The English teller has the frog demanding matter-of-factly: "Put me in your little bed." And she does. Not once, not twice, but three nights running, whereupon the frog turns into a handsome prince who gazes at the princess "with the most beautiful eyes." That marriage follows immediately proves that, by his transformation into a prince, the frog has compromised her.

The German princess is not so easily beguiled. She listens to the frog's plea, "Carry me to your room and prepare your silken bed." But it is not a proper request for a frog to make. The implications disgust her. She refuses, until her honorable but obtuse father insists. A royal word is, after all, a royal word. Marriage for princesses has nothing to do with the niceties—only with treaties. So she carries the frog upstairs and puts him in the corner, as far from her silken bed as possible. But the frog is too smart for her. He has read the fine print in the contract. "I want to rest as much as you do," he says. "Pick me up or I will tell your father." Literally matching her deed to his word, she picks him up between her thumb and forefinger, and then flings him against the wall with all her might, shouting, "Now you'll get your rest, you nasty frog." He slides down the wall and falls to the floor and turns into a handsome prince "with beautiful smiling eyes."

The so-called Green Knight variant has the frog, after three nights in the princess's bed, asking her to cut his head off. She does so with alacrity. Then he, too, turns into a prince, "with the most beautiful eyes."

Still the theme is the same: under the warty countenance, under the loathsome skin, there can still beat a princely heart. Sometimes the revelation comes after a night with the princess. Sometimes it comes with a blow to the neck or a splash against the wall. But the essence of the frog-prince story is the storyteller's belief that a loving heart could be encysted in a horrible form. Perhaps there is a cultural or historical perspective similarly hidden in the story's body, for as Iona and Peter Opie have written: "The idea that a kiss or the marriage bed could release a person from the curse of monstrousness was one that thrilled readers in the Middle Ages." It is just as thrilling for those of us in our own "middle ages" to know that we can be loved beyond our extra pounds and gray hair and wrinkled skin. Our delight in the tale carries over to the children we recite it to, and the child we still harbor within.

Besides, it is a simply wonderful feast for the Freudians, who can see in this particular story tumescence, detumescence, maidenhood, Oedipal regression, and the rest. Or one might prefer scholar Roger Sale's more cynical evaluation: "The rewards are clearly in excess of the princess's deserts..." he writes. "She *deserves* a spanking, if you like. But the strain in the story that creates this sense of unfairness is exactly what is required to overcome the fear of the repulsive object that has come to eat and sleep with the princess."

This is not simply a story about a frog and a prince. A story about a frog would be biological. A story about a prince would be historical. But a story about a frog-prince is magical and therein lies all the difference.

The magical story is not a microscope but a mirror, not a drop of water but a well. It is not simply one thing or two, but a multitude. It is at once lucid and opaque, it accepts both dark and light, speaks to youth and old age.

A reviewer writing about Isak Dinesen's tales once said that her greatest gift was that she could "accept opacities." Some critics would have us believe that opacities have no place in children's books; that a story must be transparent or apparent, that a child must not be frustrated in his or her understanding of a tale.

But to filter out the opacities for the child reader is to rob the tale of its magic. And this is a loss for the adult reader, too. If a story is totally transparent, it has no interest beyond that first reading or hearing. A fine story—whether for children or adults—should reflect both dark and light, both shadow and glare.

Look back into folklore and legend, myth and religion, and you will find much of the emphasis is on the shadow. A shadowless man is a monster, a devil, a thing of evil. A man without a shadow is soulless. A shadow without a man is a pitiable shred. Yet together, light and dark, they make a whole. And these light/dark chiaroscuro figures walking about a magical landscape illumine all our lives.

***

The familiar tale of Cinderella is another case in point. It is part of the American creed, recited subvocally along with the pledge of allegiance in each classroom, that even a poor boy can grow up to be president. And even a poor girl could grow up and become the president's wife. This unliberated corollary, this rags-to-riches formula, was immortalized in the nation's children's fiction. It is the essence of the Horatio Alger stories popular in the 1860s and of the Pluck and Luck nickel novels of the 1920s, and it has made "Cinderella" a perennial favorite in the American folktale pantheon.

But it is a wrong reading of the tale. It is wrong on two counts.

First, "Cinderella" is *not* a story of rags-to-riches, but rather of riches-to-rags-to-riches; riches recovered; a winning back of a lost patrimony. "Rumpelstiltskin," in which a miller tells a whopping lie and his docile daughter acquiesces in it in order to become a queen, seems more to the point.

Second, Cinderella, until lately, has never been a passive dreamer waiting for rescue. The forerunners of the Ash-girl have all been hardy, active heroines who take their lives into their hands and work out their own salvations. (And not without a bit of finagling and vengeance to boot.)

The story of Cinderella has endured for over a thousand years, first surfacing in a literary source in ninth-century China. It has since been found from the Orient to the interior of South America, and over five hundred variants have been located by folklorists in

33

Europe alone. This best-beloved tale has been brought to life over and over so many times, no one can say for sure where the oral tale truly began. But as Joseph Jacobs, the indefatigable Victorian collector, once said of a Cinderella story he printed, it was "an English version of an Italian adaptation of a Spanish translation of a Latin version of a Hebrew translation of an Arabic translation of an Indian original." That is certainly an accurate statement of the hazards of folktale attributing: each reteller has brought to a tale something of his or her cultural orientation. The Chinese admiration for the tiny "lotus foot" is preserved in the Cinderella tale, as is the seventeenth-century European preoccupation with dressing for the ball.

But beyond the cultural accoutrements, the detritus of centuries, Cinderella speaks to all of us in whatever skin we inhabit: the child mistreated, a princess or highborn lady in disguise bearing her trials with patience, fortitude, and determination. Cinderella makes intelligent decisions, for she knows that wishing solves nothing without the concomitant action. We have each of us been that child. (Even boys and men share that dream, as evidenced by the many Ash-boy variants.) It is the longing of any youngster sent supperless to bed or given less than a full share at Christmas. And of course it is the adolescent dream.

To make Cinderella less than she is, an ill-treated but passive princess awaiting her rescue, cheapens our most cherished dreams and makes a mockery of the magic inside us all—the ability to change our own lives, the ability to control our own destinies.

In the oldest of the Cinderella variants, the heroine is hardly catatonic. In the Grimm "Cinder-Maid," though she weeps, she continues to perform the proper rites and rituals at her mother's grave, instructing the birds who roost there in the way to help her get to the ball. In the "Dirty Shepherdess" variant and "Cap o' Rushes" from France, "...she dried her eyes, and made a bundle of her jewels and her best dresses and hurriedly left the castle where she was born." Off she goes to make her own life, working first as a maid in the kitchen and sneaking off to see the master's son. Even in Perrault's seventeenth-century "Cendrillon, or The Little Glass Slipper," when the fairy godmother runs out of ideas for enchantment, and was at a loss for a coachman, "I'll go and see," says Cendrillon, "if there be never a rat in the rat-trap, we'll make a coach-man of him."

The older Cinderella is no namby-pamby forgiving heroine. Like Chesterton's children, who believe themselves innocent and demand justice—unlike adults who know themselves guilty and look for mercy—Cinderella believes in justice. In "Rushen Coatie" and "The Cinder-Maid," the elder sisters hack off their toes and heels in order to try and fit the tiny shoe, and Cinderella never stops them. Her tattletale birds warn the prince:

> Turn and peep, turn and peep,
> There's blood within the shoe;
> A bit is cut from off the heel
> And a bit from off the toe.

Does Cinderella comfort her maimed sisters? Nary a word. And, in the least bowdlerized of the German and Nordic variants, when the two sisters attend the wedding of Cinderella and the prince, "the elder was at the right side and the younger at the left, and the pigeons pecked out one eye from each of them." Did Cinderella stop the carnage—or the wedding? There is never a misstep between that sentence and the next. "Afterwards, as they came back, the elder was on the left, and the younger on the right, and then the pigeons pecked out the other eye from each. And thus, for their wickedness and falsehood, they were punished with blindness all their days."

Of course, all this went into the Walt Disney blender and came out emotional pap. In 1950, when the movie *Cinderella* burst onto the American scene, the Disney studios were going through a particularly trying time. Disney had been deserted by the intellectuals who had championed his art for some time. Because of World War II, the public had been more interested in war films than cartoons. But with the release of *Cinderella,* the Disney studios made a fortune, grossing $4.247 million in the first release alone. It set a new pattern for Cinderella: a helpless, hapless, pitiable, useless heroine who has to be saved time and time again by the talking mice and birds because she is "off in a world of dreams." It is a Cinderella who is not recognized by her prince until she is magically back in her ball gown, beribboned and bejeweled.

Poor Cinderella. Poor us. The acculturation of millions of boys and girls to this passive Cinderella robs the old tale of its invigorating magic. The story has been falsified and the true meaning lost—perhaps forever.

The Eye and the Ear

Once upon a time, a long time ago, there was a child who loved to listen to stories. And one summer night, in a cottage in Maine, the child sat in an audience of other children and adults while a storyteller recounted the history of a Greek hero named Perseus.

And when the storyteller came to the part where the hero held up the head of the gorgon Medusa, she held her own hand aloft. I could have sworn then—as I can swear now—that I saw snakes from the gorgon's head curling and uncurling around the storyteller's arm.

At that moment I and all the other listeners around me were unable to move. It was as if we, and not Medusa's intended victims, had been turned to stone.

It could have been a trick of the firelight behind the storyteller. It might have been the hot dogs I had hastily consumed before trotting over from our cottage, my little sandals slip-slapping on the stony beach walk. It might have been the lateness of the hour or my overactive imagination. But I know that it was none of these. It was simply the power of the teller and the tale.

We were there, all of us, caught up in the centrifugal force of the spinning story. And we would not be let go until the teller finished and the tale was done.

Of course the story in the mouth is different from the one on the page. The tale apprehended by the ear is different from the one taken in by the eye.

Critic Jack Schaefer states baldly: "Literature is a maimed art, crippled by being printed in books." Though it is true that there is a silent intimidation of print that frightens some children and some adults, I would rather say it this way: *The eye and the ear are different listeners.*

What sounds well at night by a listening child's bed does not read as well on the page. What lies perfectly formed in Bodoni Bold on the white sheet may stutter on the tongue tomorrow. I could never write down and make a book of the stories of the absurd "Silly Gorilly" which entertained my three children through years of bedtime telling. How can I recapture my own lumbering gallop around the room, the infection of giggles shared, the pauses, the tickles, the rolling of eyes? On the other hand, how does one deal with sight rhymes like rain/again or wind/kind, rhymes that resonate to the eye but do not work well on a twenty-first-century American tongue? In bookmaking, one must try to please the ear as well as the eye, but it is often a compromise.

There is a subtle play of text and type, illustrations and design, that can change a story just as surely as a new telling. In science, when one puts a specimen on a slide, there is a change in the specimen. So, too, putting a tale onto a page and dressing it up with full-color illustrations provokes a transformation.

Some critics, like Bruno Bettelheim, would have us do without any pictures for the fairy tales. But illustrations are well within the tradition of storytelling. Shamans and seers often accompanied their tellings with drawings, dolls, or puppets. In countries where oral tellings still exist, remnants of picture-tales exist, too. In Brazil, storytellers in villages often hang appropriate pictures on a clothesline to illustrate their story. In Arab bazaars, tale tellers make paintings of colored sand as they recite. And while it is true that pictures can change a listener's understanding of a story, so have centuries of retellers.

How much can an illustration change our hearing of a tale? Just look at three different versions of "Snow White" and it is easy to see.

Randall Jarrell's retelling of the Grimm story has full-color pictures by Nancy Ekholm Burkert. They emphasize the medieval setting. Her queen is a professional necromancer, a potent potion-maker, whose *grimoire* is filled with evil recipes. The queen's picture is set about with crucibles, tarot cards, hanging herbs. But we never see her face. And so the old prototype of faceless evil is presented to us.

Burkert's Snow White, on the other hand, we see full face on the jacket and beyond. She is so fair of face as to be translucent, otherworldly, reminiscent of the Victorian child saints. Yet she is healthy enough, light-footed and sure with the forest animals; housewifely (almost homely) in her turban as she cooks and cleans for the dwarves. She is seen as saint, as child, as homemaker, the three faces of archetypal woman.

The backgrounds are millefleurs tapestries, recalling the wall hangings of the period.

The dwarves are fully human and therefore pitiable in their role as deformed humanity. The prince and Snow White are innocents, with the faces of children but the bodies of adults. The dwarves have adult faces on which the loss of innocence shows, but they are small and childlike, too. They are midway between the full-face innocence of Snow White and the faceless evil of the queen.

No words intrude upon Nancy Burkert's allegorical presentation. The text is set apart by itself: two pages of text, two pages of illustration. It is fascinating bookmaking, capturing the penumbral side of the tale. It asks questions rather than answers them. It enunciates the archetypes.

Trina Schart Hyman's "Snow White," on the other hand, is firmly rooted in humanity. The faces she pictures are real faces: Snow White is her own daughter Katrin. The Queen is an old friend. Hyman is one of the dwarves herself; the others include her ex-husband and her neighbors in New Hampshire. Portraiture is Hyman's forte.

Her prince is bearded, hawk-nosed, strong-featured, in his thirties. He is the only prince in "Snow White" illustrations who looks as though he knows how to run a kingdom and deal with wicked stepmothers, and he is just waiting for his chance. No beardless adolescent this, no sweet-faced youth just out of knickers. The red-hot iron shoes at the end of the story must be *his* idea.

From the opening scene in Trina Hyman's "Snow White," where the girl is seen in a flash-forward hanging out dwarf-sized shirts to dry on the line, this is a less regal, more human book. Ms. Hyman is fascinated not by archetypes but by the play of light and dark, good and evil in faces. Even the queen's mirror is ringed with them, faces that shift and direct mood for the reader. Hyman's precursors are the Pre-Raphaelites, Wyeth, and Pyle, and she combines sweetness and toughness to offer up an illustrated tale. The text, translated by Paul Heins, is incorporated into the pictures.

Hyman's concerns are immediate, human, sensual. The queen radiates a power that is sexual in nature. The story told by Trina Hyman is the Electra story. We can see it in the faces, we can see the palpable sexuality in the form of the mandrake root that hangs symbolically from the queen's wall. The laces that the queen binds around the innocent Snow White bind her into a caricature of a full-bosomed peasant girl and the dwarves look at the sleeping girl, so bound, with a hint of carnality. Quite simply, Ms. Hyman makes you hear the tale anew.

Walt Disney, on the other hand, sentimentalizes everything in his version of the story, flattens out both the text and the illustrations to cartoon caricatures. His wicked queen is neither the faceless sorceress of legend nor the decaying beauty, but a cartoon witch, with nose and chin threatening to meet. She loses depth, motive, individuality, and so never achieves the power of Burkert's herbalist or Hyman's voluptuary, and she does not die but merely disappears conveniently, in a Perils-of-Pauline ending, "into a bottomless gulf."

So, too, the dwarves lose their power and place in the Disney story by becoming cute, providing that measure of "adorableness" that, as critic Richard Schickel puts it, "was the most persistent problem of Disney's work."

With both her nemesis and her collective alter egos robbed of their power and depth, Snow White herself is left with nothing to resound against. Without true evil, there is little excitement, no contrasting background against which to dramatize virtue. The story becomes, in this telling, a hollow tale. The Disney version illustrates with finality folklorist Mircea Eliade's contention that "Man's concept of the absolute can never be uprooted; it can only be debased."

Disney was a man who believed that we "recognize [good and evil] instinctively..." and he supposed that any retellings of fairy tales could be approached in this simplistic manner. But the power of the tales is that they are not that simple after all. They are as evocative, as sensual, as many-faceted, as disturbing, as slippery as dreams. They offer a moral, they speak to the human condition, but it is not always the condition or the moral one immediately sees.

That is why a fine artist can bring to an old tale a new approach, a new direction. Nancy Ekholm Burkert's "Snow White" is a different story from Trina Schart Hyman's. And they are both completely different tales from Walt Disney's oversimplification. If a story were rewritten in succession by John Gardner, Isaac Bashevis Singer, and Dr. Seuss—how different each story would be.

The eye and the ear are different listeners. Each storyteller has the ability to select: to select those characters who are just right, to select those details that set the stage, to select the glass mountain that must be climbed, the thorny bush that must be passed or the ring or sword or crown to be won. The storyteller is an artist, and selection is essential to art. There are thousands upon thousands of characters, thousands upon thousands of details, thousands upon thousands of motifs. To know which one to choose requires a kind of magical touch, and that is what characterizes the great storytellers.

But the eye and the ear are different listeners. The modern audience is not the same as the ancient one, and for good reason. Ancient man took in the world mainly by listening, and listening meant remembering. Thus humans both shaped and were shaped by the oral tradition. The passage of culture went from mouth to ear to mouth. The person who did not listen well, who was tone deaf to the universe, was soon dead. The finest rememberers and the most attuned listeners were valued: the poets, the storytellers, the shamans, the seers. In culture after culture, community after community, the carriers of the oral tradition were honored. For example, in ancient Ireland the *ollahms,* the poet-singers, were more highly thought of than the king. The king was only given importance in times of war.

An anthropologist friend of mine once observed that people in preliterate cultures that are still more of the ear than the eye say, "I hear you," when they mean they understand something. But we say, "I see." We modern listeners see life more clearly through pictures. We trust the picture more than the spoken word. A picture, we are told, is worth a thousand words. In the last century we created the moving picture and credit it, more than anything else, with shaping our children's thoughts.

But the eye and the ear are different listeners, are different audiences. And the literary storyteller is one who must try to bring eye and ear into synchronization. But it is a subtle art. Just as the art of typography has been called "the art invisible," subliminal in the sense that it changes or manipulates a reader's perceptions without advertising its own presence, so, too, the art of storytelling in the printed book must persuade and captivate. It must hold the reader as the spoken tale holds the listener, turning the *body* to stone but not the mind or the heart.

Touch Magic

Every few decades, with a regularity that suggests a natural cycle, the fairy tale haters arrive. Under the banner of reason, they blast away with their howitzers at the little singing bird of faerie.

Ever since St. Jerome, who considered such poetic stuff "the food of demons," the haters have played their off-key tune, trying to pipe Pan out of the garden. And whether it was Mrs. Trimmer warning against "the danger as well as the impropriety of putting such books in the hands of little children whose minds are susceptible of every impression…" or the well-meaning Gradgrind who wrote in the 1960s in the *London Times Literary Supplement* that fairy stories "ultimately contribute to a more general alienation, a preference for living wholly in dreams and an inability to face reality," the legionnaires of reason have been marching on the right track but in the wrong direction. They would have us believe, as in the old Danish nursery rhyme:

> Oh it is not the fault of the hen
> That the cock is dead,
> It is the fault of the nightingale
> Within the green garden.

The wrong singer is blamed. It is quite definitely *not* the nightingale, the sweet singer, who contributes to alienation. Point the finger, instead, at those down-to-earth hen stories that claim to be about the here-and-now but are, however, so unlike anyone's true existence that they can mislead and misrepresent real life to a reader.

It is true that fairy tales have an effect, but it is a healthy, nurturing, cathartic effect, not a fault. Using archetypes and symbolic language, they externalize for the listener conflicts and situations that cannot be spoken of or explained or as yet analyzed. They give substance to dreams.

Folklore is, in part, the history of humankind. And we share fears, hopes, joys with our apelike ancestors who prayed to the sun and hid from the stars. As Ursula Le Guin has written, "…we all have the same kind of dragons in our psyche, just as we all have the same kind of hearts and lungs in our body."

Folklore is, of course, imperfect history because it is history constantly transforming and being transformed, putting on, chameleonlike, the colors of its background. But while it is imperfect history, it is the perfect guidebook to the human psyche; it leads us to the understanding of the deepest longings and most daring visions of humankind.

The images from the ancients speak to us in modern tongue though we may not always grasp the "meanings" consciously. Like dreams, the meanings slip away, leaving us shaken into new awarenesses. We are moved by them even when—or perhaps *because*—we do not understand them on the conscious level. They are penumbral, partially lit, and it is the dark side that has the most power.

So when the modern mythmaker, the writer of literary fairy tales, dares to touch the old magic and try to make it work in new ways, it must be done with the surest of touches. It is, perhaps, a kind of artistic thievery, this stealing of old characters, settings, the accoutrements of magic. But, then, in a sense, there is an element of theft in all art; even the most imaginative artist borrows and reconstructs the archetypes when delving into the human heart. That is not to say that using a familiar character from folklore in hopes of shoring up a weak narrative will work. That makes little sense. Unless the image, character, or situation borrowed speaks to the author's condition, as cryptically and oracularly as a dream, folklore is best left untapped.

Some examples from my own stories may serve to demonstrate the blending of folkloric elements with original themes to create the literary or art tale.

The Bird of Time is such a collage. I began the story when I misheard some rock lyrics. It was related also to a distant memory of the *Rubáiyát of Omar Khayyám* I had been given as a child, with the multifaceted pictures by Edmund Dulac.

> Come into the fire of Spring
> Your winter garment of repentance fling.
> The bird of time has but a little way to flutter,
> And lo! the bird is on the wing.

The story has a traditional son setting out to seek his traditional fortune. Every folk culture boasts numbers of such tales. In my story the hero was also able to understand the language of beasts and birds. You can find such prodigies aplenty in folklore: the Norwegian lad in "The Giant Who Had No Heart in His Body" is one; the Bulgarian boy in "The Snake King's Gift" and the German hero of "Faithful John" (one of my childhood favorites) are others.

But *The Bird of Time* also had a theme of my own devising, and the theme came straight out of my own life. It happened that I began the story when my beloved mother was dying of cancer. In fact, the very day when I wrote the first words of the tale was the day I learned of her condition. Yet such is the ability of the subconscious mind to work out trauma, I did not realize this coincidence of time until months later.

In the story, I wrote of a wonder: a bird that could magically alter time, slowing it down, speeding it up, or stopping time altogether. If I could not do such a thing in real life to save my mother, I could certainly do it where I had total control: on the pages of a book.

Months later, when the story was done, I let my mother read the tale in manuscript. (She was not to live to see the finished book, which was dedicated to her.) Only then did I learn how much of me was in the story. I can still see her as she was that day, a small, intense, dark-haired woman sitting in a large brown leather chair. Her legs were curled up under her, her favorite reading position. And when she finished reading, she looked up at me over her glasses and said, "Intimations of mortality, eh?" And smiled.

It was then I knew that she knew she was dying, though my father had been desperate to keep the fact of her cancer from her. And I knew, for the first time, what my little story was all about.

***

Perhaps art imitates life. Sometimes, though, art aids life. These kinds of tales, which are crafted visions, printed dreams, are also a working-out of thematic materials in an artist's life. In that way, then, these kinds of stories are the best "problem-solvers," the truest kinds of tales. In the story "The Boy Who Sang For Death" in my collection *Dream Weaver,* I came to terms at last with my mother's death.

The story was the last one I wrote for the collection and was begun at an art auction. I was attending it with my editor, and in between the auctioneer's sales, she and I were discussing the book. It lacked something, she said. It was a book about dreams, but it lacked the dream about Death.

"I know what it is!" I whispered loudly, throwing up one hand. Inadvertently I purchased a painting at the same time, for the auctioneer took my raised arm as a bid.

The idea I had had in that instant was visual. I saw a mountain pass and a line of dead soldiers lined up behind a beautiful girl dressed in white—Death. And the line was stopped because a young man was dancing. The title was in my head, too, "The Boy Who Danced For Death." I had spent many years studying ballet, first at the Balanchine school in New York City and later on with another Russian emigré teacher in Connecticut. And though by the time of the auction I was too old and too fat to be a dancer, my inner self still danced. If anything could stop Death, my image-self said, it was Dance. (And perhaps I was remembering, too, the Dance of Death from the medieval paintings and stories.)

But when I came to write the tale, the dancer did not stay with me. Because before dancing—and after—in my life there is music. I am a singer, and have used the magical power of music in my stories before. So the dancer became transmuted into a singer.

I wrote the story in a white heat and finished it in five days after the *singer* appeared. Then I read it aloud to myself in my kitchen. (I read all my stories aloud, for these are out of the oral tradition by way of print and they are meant to be heard.)

And then I came to the line, spoken by the singer, whose mother has died: "Any gift I have I would surely give to get my mother back."

I had written the story. I had written that line. But it was as if I had not understood it before. In my kitchen, at midday, with the sun streaming in over my shoulders, I began to cry. The story was an exorcism, an expiation, a final present for my mother, dead eight years.

***

Diane Wolkstein, who is a great storyteller, has written that when she tells stories to an audience she knows that not every story will strike that kind of chord with every listener. But she can tell, just by the faces, when she has hit *the* story for a particular person. And that is because the listener is immobilized, paralyzed by hearing his or her particular truth being spoken aloud.

These are the kinds of tales that force a confrontation with the deepest kind of reality. In Tolkien's words, these tales give the child "the very taste of primary truth."

I have seen this healing and revealing power of folktale demonstrated clearly within the context of my own family. Our cat Pod, a beautiful golden tom, was killed, rather brutally, by unleashed dogs running wild in our field. The children witnessed the whole thing, and by the time I was able to drive the dogs off, and gather my children, Pod was dead. His golden fur was muddy and mauled, his eyes wide, his once lithe body stiff.

We made an elaborate funeral with singing and prayers and wildflowers to cover him: milkweed fluff and Quaker ladies, Queen Anne's lace, king devil, and rye. We sang him a farewell song, and Heidi and Jason, ages ten and six, were able to sob their goodbyes.

47

But Adam, then age eight, was stony-faced. It was not that he had loved Pod any more or any less. He just would not come to Pod's grave. And he could not cry.

For two days he remained unreachable, his grief held behind a set jaw. He would not talk about it, he barely ate, he would not play with the others. And he could not cry.

The second evening I sat down with the three to read them a fairy tale, one that I loved: the Grimms' story, "Goose Girl," a Cinderella variant. In it, the girl's magical companion, the horse Falada, is ritually killed and its head is hung up over the arched gateway to advise her. As the goose girl walks under the door, she looks up and cries out, "Alas, Falada, hanging there."

When I reached that point in the tale, Adam burst into tears. He sobbed for a long time. And when at last he calmed down, he asked me, "Why can I cry at that story when I couldn't at Pod's death?"

Why indeed? I told him that it had to do with that inner core of "primary truth," only I didn't put it exactly that way. I told him that though life and art are not really imitations, one of another, they resonate. At that particular moment in his particular young life, Adam had found *his* tale.

Did I know all this before I chose that story? A little, perhaps. I was a mother and a storyteller, and also a bit desperate to reach my child.

All I know is that after that, Adam went outside to the cat's grave that he had dared not visit before.

***

Falada was not real and Pod was. Yet within the body of the story was a truth that spoke out loud and clear to one grieving little boy. It reminds me, years later, of the truth about dinosaurs and dragons.

Though we are just now finding out that the dinosaur was probably a warm-blooded beast and not the cold-blooded lizard of the textbooks, we have never been in doubt about dragons. We know, even without being told, that they were born, nourished, kept alive by human blood and heart and mind. They never were—but always will be. It was Kenneth Grahame who wrote: "The dragon is a more enduring animal than a pterodactyl. I have never yet met anyone who really believed in a pterodactyl; but every honest person believes in dragons—down in the back-kitchen of his consciousness."

Dragons and pterodactyls, actuality has nothing to do with Truth.

Throughout the nineteenth century, there was a great deal of speculation about fairies. One group of anthropologists and folklorists held that there really had been a race of diminutive prehistoric people who had been driven underground by successive invasions. These "little folk," who were really about the size of pygmies, supposedly lived for years in communities in caves and burrows, in warrens and tunnels and in the deepest, darkest parts of the forest where, in brown-and-green camouflage, they stayed apart from their enemies. Kidnapings and mysterious disappearances were all attributed to them. These hardy guerrillas of a defeated culture became, in the folk mind, the elves and gnomes and trolls and fairies of the British Isles. There were even archeologists who were convinced they had discovered rooms underground in the Orkney Islands that resembled the Elfland of the popular ballad *Child Rowland*. (And similarly, other such folk stories might have emerged by a misunderstanding of the weirs and dikes used by the Romans for their household baths.)

It is a very seductive thesis, but it really begs the question. For even if we do conclusively prove that the Picts or Celts or some other smaller-than-average race are the *actual* precursors of the fairy folk, it will not really change a thing about those wonderful stories. The tales of Elfland do not stand or fall on their actuality but on their truthfulness, their speaking to the human condition, the longings we all have for the Faerie Other. Those are the tales that touch our longing for the better, brighter world; our shared myths, our shaped dreams. The fears and longings within each of us that helped us create Heaven and Elysium, Valhalla and Tir nan og.

This is the stuff that dreams are made of. Not the smaller dreams that you and I have each night, rehearsals of things to come, anticipation or dread turned into murky symbols, pastiches of traumas just passed. These are the larger dreams of humankind, a patchwork of all the smaller dreams stitched together by time.

The best of the stories we can give our children, whether they are stories that have been kept alive through the centuries by that mouth-to-mouth resuscitation we call oral transmission, or the tales that were made up only yesterday—the best of these stories touch that larger dream, that greater vision, that infinite unknowing. They are the most potent kind of magic, these tales, for they catch a glimpse of the soul beneath the skin.

Touch magic. Pass it on.

PART TWO
Taradiddles

The Mask on the Lapel

In eighteenth-century Venice, when masked balls were a common pastime, it became a convention that anyone wearing a mask remained unrecognized. From this grew another custom. Someone wishing to go out into the street disguised need only wear a symbolic miniature mask in a buttonhole to be considered incognito. That tiny pin was always respected. The wearer was then immune from censorious eyes. The pin said, in effect, "I am not I," and the person behind the pin was free to act the stranger, the commoner, the charlatan, the fool. Any evening became carnival, any man or woman a player in his or her own elaborate pantomime.

In a very real sense, the author of a fantasy book wears a mask on the lapel. The act of inventing a new world, or investing this one with wonders, sets the tone for "I am not I." For obviously this is not the actual or real world if animals can converse, trees dance, or people ride about on dragons. It is a land where the taradiddle, the fancy, the elaborated lie is king. And yet...and yet the talking beasts, the ballet of birch and oak, the riders of the wind are another way of presenting the real world. And the reader—child or adult— who learns to use eyes and ears and mind and heart in this manner can never again took at the world in a one-dimensional way.

A child who can love the oddities of a fantasy book cannot possibly be xenophobic as an adult. What is a different color, a different culture, a different tongue for a child who has already mastered Elvish, respected Puddleglums, or fallen under the spell of dark-skinned Ged, the greatest wizard Earthsea has ever known?

And for adults, the world of fantasy books returns to us the great words of power that, in order to be tamed, have been excised from our adult vocabularies. These words are the pornography of innocence, words that adults no longer dare to use with other adults, and so we laugh at them and consign them to the nursery, fear masking as cynicism. These are the words that were forged in the earth, air, fire, and water of human existence. And the words are:

Good.
Evil.
Courage.
Honor.
Truth.
Hate.
Love.

They are a litany, a charm so filled with power we hardly dare say them. Yet with those magical words, anything is possible: the transformation of human into beast, dead into living, night into day, year now into year then or year 3000. They are the stuff of which our visions are woven, the warp and weft of our crafted dreams.

Literature, of course, is an unnatural act committed by two consenting individuals—writer and reader. Or, as Joyce Cary once wrote, "Reading is a creative art subject to the same rules, the same limitations, as the imaginative process." But for the fantasy writer, the paramount need is for a creative reader, an active participant in that unnatural act. Each—writer and reader—helps create the world. The pattern is the book. A fantasy novel is more than an adventure or a quest. Rather it is a series of image-repeating glasses, a hall of mirrors that brings past and future into focus and calls it the present.

The fantasy story is a story of magic. But let us play with words for a moment. First take the magician, or as he was known in the days of swords and sorcery, the *mage*. The mage was a person of great wisdom and learning that some call evil and some call good.

The mage had his *magic,* which is the art of producing, by leger-demain or optical illusion, surprising phenomena and seemingly unnatural effects. In short, he produces *images* that pass for reality, that change our understanding of what is real, that push us past our initial perceptions into the world of *imagination.*

Mage.
Magic.
Image.
Imagination.

Albert Einstein said, "Imagination is more important than knowledge." And in what literature, that bond between writer and reader, do you find the template for imagination more palpable than in a fantasy book?

The fantasy novel presents a world of poetry, of dream-making and sometimes of dream-breaking.

Anyone saying of it, "This world as I tell it to you *actually* exists," would (and possibly should) be carted off to an institution. And yet there were and are those for whom Hades and the Isles of the Blessed and Qudlivun are vividly real. And Heaven. And Hell. A world in which justice and mercy go hand in hand. Where the streets are paved with gold. Where a poor man or woman could become president—or king. Such fantasy is another word for reality then, another word for the hope and the dream.

So the fantasy book, like the fairy tale, may not be Life Actual but it *is* Life in Truth.

Life Actual tells us that the world is not perfectly ordered; it is, in fact, most often immoral or anyway amoral. Endings are as often unhappy as happy. Issues are seldom clear-cut. Judgment is as capri-cious as justice. Babies starve and there is no resurrecting them. Mothers die or run off and are never found. Families are torn asun-der and there is no mending them. And honesty is rarely the best policy when it comes to exposing your friends. That is Life Actual.

But Life in Truth tells us something else. It tells us of the world *as it should be.* It holds certain values to be important. It makes issues clear. It is, if you will, a fiction based on great opposites, the clashing of opposing forces, question and answer, speech and echo, yin and yang, the great dance of opposites. And so the fantasy tale, the "I that is not I," becomes a rehearsal for the reader for life as it *should* be lived.

That sounds terribly religious. At the least, it is awfully moral and faintly innocent, certainly naive. It makes a lot of adults uncomfortable, so they relegate this literature to the nursery, along with the fairy tale from whose loins the fantasy story sprang.

Do not be so beguiled. There is an extra coin that must be paid when crossing the Styx of the imagination. E. M. Forster recognized this in his *Aspects of the Novel,* saying: "What does fantasy ask of us? It asks us to pay something extra. It compels us to an adjustment that is different to an adjustment required by a work of art, to an additional adjustment." And the extra coin, the "additional adjustment," is this: for the moment the reader must accept the mask on the lapel. For the moment, the reader must not challenge the author, must not recognize the recognizable human face above the buttonhole. The reader must step into the new world, partake of its wonders, assuming for the moment that they *are* real.

Just as the hero in Chesterton's essay "The Dragon's Grandmother" knows that the world is full of marvels but the soul of man is sane, so, too, the hero of a fantasy book goes through the most incredible situations, never taking time to look around and say, "This cannot be. There really *are* no such things as dragons, trolls, rats conversing in boats, or walking trees." Such a statement would break the bubble-dream of story. Accept the possibility of wonder and you accept the possibility of heroism. After all, Bilbo and Frodo Baggins *became* heroes because they forged ahead, not because they were born heroic.

One of my children retained his fear of huge, horrible monsters in our dark upstairs hall well into his eleventh year. Yet he told me, when I suggested putting shades on his window to shut out some of the more terrifying shadows the great pine tree threw on his walls at night, "No, in some ways that tree is my friend. I wave at it before I go to bed, and it waves back. I don't think I want shades. I think I prefer the shadows."

Perceptive child. Preferring the shadows is another way of accepting opacities. Accepting the possibility of the dark means accepting the possibility of the light. All the best and toughest tales of magic share this double-natured universe. In the fantasy world, that duality is clear.

In our Actual world, of course, evil often comes wearing a benign face, a smiling countenance, even a clown's nose. In what fantasy world would we ever permit an oven cleaner commercial on a TV show about the Holocaust? In what fantasy world would we make the villain a failed sign painter with a silly mustache? In what fantasy world would we permit a full-color presentation of a president's assassination to be broadcast again and again, his brains being splattered in slow motion just at lunchtime?

Life is not art, and we may be thankful for that. And art is not life, just tidier. Begun as a dream or a vision, the fantasy book moves beyond dreams and into craft. And there it is polished until it shines, ready for its audience, which is many miles wide and many years deep.

Sometimes, of course, the audience is not ready for it. There is a story that is told about William Morris, who sent his friend Rossetti a presentation copy of his newest book, *Sigurd the Volsung*. Morris waited many days hoping to hear from Rossetti, if not praises, at least an acknowledgment that the book had actually arrived. But not a word came.

Finally Morris charged over to Rossetti's studio where he found the painter in the middle of stretching a canvas.

"Evidently," Morris shouted, "you did not like my book or you would have written to me about it."

Never looking up from the canvas, Rossetti replied, "To tell the truth, I must own that I find it difficult to take much interest in a man whose father was a dragon."

But Morris had the last word. "I don't see that it's any odder than having a brother who's an idiot!" he shouted, and stormed from the room.

Every person's father is a dragon—and also a dragon slayer, the two eternal opposites. Only very special fathers have the ability to integrate the two sides, and only very special children can actually see that integration. Mother and stepmother, godmother and witch, hero and villain, over and over the contrapuntal dance goes on. And so the children in their turn become dragons—and dragon slayers.

That is why stories about dragons, about heroes, about the other worlds, speak so strongly to us, adults and children, in whatever skin we inhabit. As Ursula Le Guin writes, "They speak *from* the unconscious *to* the unconscious, in the *language* of the unconscious—symbol and archetype..."

The fantasy novel speaks many times to the listener. Once in the ear, and again and again and again in the echo chamber that is the heart.

Tough Magic

Children have always been attracted to magic. One year, with a kit they bought from a toy store, my children presented a living room sleight-of-hand show. It had a mistress of ceremonies, audience participation, and even an encore. Everything, in fact, but magic.

A few days later I was buying an airplane ticket and noticed a brightly colored poster portraying some very familiar Disney characters capering around a pair of aging tourists. The poster urged: *To Reach The Magic Kingdom, Call Your Travel Agent.*

So much for magic today: tricks from a kit and an airplane ride. I must admit I miss the very different magic of my own childhood: the cry of the wind over English moors I had never visited, the dusky callings of seabirds circling pirate ships on the Spanish Main, the death song of a knight's sword as it whistled through the still air, the incantations crooned over fires and witches' cauldrons. Instead of shapeshifters laboriously changing their forms under the eye of the gibbous moon, there are the instantaneous transformations and dissolves of television, the easy trickery of the tube. What do the children know today of Tough Magic?

Tough Magic. It is the old bargain principle. One cannot receive without first giving. Every miracle requires an initial disaster.

Magic has consequences. That kind of wisdom can be found in the best of the old tales: Prometheus offering fire and receiving the vulture at his breast. Arthur pulling the sword from the stone and receiving along with it a kingdom full of troubles. Beauty nearly killing her father for want of a rose and nearly killing the Beast for want of her father. And in one of the Grimms' best tales, "Faithful John," John saves his master the king by speaking himself into stone while the king, in turn, has to cut the throats of his own beloved children if the stone is ever to become human again.

As Chesterton wrote: "[In the old tales] one idea runs from one end of them to the other—the idea that peace and happiness can only exist on some condition. This idea, which is the core of ethics, is the core of the nursery tale." You can never get without giving. The fantasy story that best illustrates this idea is one that Ursula Le Guin wrote called "The Ones Who Walk Away From Omelas." In it, a perfect society exists only on the precondition that one child, one chosen child, is treated subhumanly down in a dark dungeon. This shadow-side, this hideous Other, is the price the inhabitants must pay. But some folk will not pay with another's horrible life, and those are the very few who walk away from their perfect land. It is a masterful tale.

Tough Magic. The good sister in the old tale helps out without thought of reward and is given a mouthful of diamonds. The bad sister goes looking for diamonds and gets toads. A condition of choice overlies the best stories and that is what is missing in so much of the new literature for children. Instead of that reminder of the hard work of choosing, we are each of us told we can marry the prince or princess. The half of the kingdom is ours for the asking. There is never the risk of a mouthful of toads.

Tough Magic usually asks as its price the utmost sacrifice: a life, a soul, a never-ending torture. And those who choose Tough Magic never really know whether the ultimate rescue is at hand. The outcome is always in doubt at the moment of choosing. Prometheus knows he must endure until a son of Zeus arrives, but he does not know when that will be. Arthur waits in Avalon, neither dead nor alive, until he is needed again in the world, betrayed but not forgotten. Beauty would wed her Beast in his loathsome form, never guessing a prince's face lies hidden beneath the hideous skin. Faithful John and his master's children do survive, but we learn that only in the final paragraphs of the tale. And so the tensions of the stories carry us past the unbelievability of the magic into the credibility of miracles in our everyday lives.

Without Tough Magic none of us can truly believe. To wish and to receive just for the wishing is too simple—and too simple-minded. There is nothing to be gained from hearing such an undemanding tale. Just to say, as the fisherman's wife does in the old story, "Make me the King, make me the Pope, make me God on his golden throne," and expect it to be without consequences, is to court disaster.

And after all, it is not the expectation of a happy ending that carries us on. Rather it is the unraveling of the story itself; it is the traveling and not the destination. In C. S. Lewis's wonderful science fantasy novel *Perelandra,* the Green Lady says: "The world is much larger than I thought...I thought we went along paths—but it seems there are no paths. The going itself is a path."

Taking that unmarked path is the way of Tough Magic. Without going that way, there is no hope of the true Happy Ever After, or what Tolkien calls the "Eucatastrophe," the joy behind the shadow. The same rule greets us in every age, in every mythology: without evil and the knowledge of its possible continuance, there can be no hope for redemption. That is what every memorable story, every tale of dimension is about: the working through evil in order to come at last to the light.

That struggle can be exemplified in the haunting cry of the hobbit Frodo in *The Lord of the Rings*. Struggling across the oppressive pits of Mordor under the burden of the magical Ring, he calls out: "No taste of food, no feel of water, no sound of wind, no memory of trees or grass or flower, no image of moon or star are left to me. I am naked in the dark...and there is no veil between me and the wheel of fire." Poor Frodo. He is totally lost, terribly afraid, *but he goes on.* Without that fear, without the threat of utter loss, what good are all the hosannahs and hallelujahs? Unless in a story an unlikely hero or heroine dares to take the last chance, the hard path unknowing, stoops to bear the burden of a magic too hard to bear, saying as Frodo does, "I will take [it] though I do not know the way," then the story loses its power to move us.

Stories of Tough Magic are never easy stories, nor should they be. As they call upon the possible sacrifice of hero or heroine, they ask a similar sacrifice on the reader's part. "Hold on," they cry out. "Delve deep," they call. "Dare to reach out and touch the face of the unknown."

In this day of easy memory and instant mnemonics, computer retrieval and the Tube, we ask very little of our children. Like that neurotic tree in Shel Silverstein's popular sado-masochistic allegory *The Giving Tree*, all is given and nothing is asked in return. So the difficult, Tough Magic stories are not always the popular ones. They ask the reader to bring as much to the tale as the writer. They force a confrontation with a harsher, deeper, truer reality. They ask heart—and give it in return.

The reader knows that she or he is the alter ego of the main character in the book, but she or he can always turn the page or close the cover if the going gets rough. But Tough Magic does not allow that choice to surface consciously. The reader, caught in the tale, spun by the centripetal force of the story, is pulled back inside his or her own brain and is unable to get free of the spell. And then it takes great courage indeed to cross Mordor with Frodo. It takes great courage to touch the dead body of Aslan upon the slab in *The Lion, the Witch and the Wardrobe*. It takes great courage to step aboard the little boat with Sparrowhawk in *A Wizard of Earthsea*. Yet in the end, this borrowed cup of courage, this acting out in fantasy, frees the reader from the fear of failing, the fear of powerlessness, the fear of fearfulness and shame. And if the reader is a child, what lessons—that awful word taken back from the Victorians who condemned fanciful tales—are learned there. The fantasy book pushes the reader on to a confrontation with life's greatest mysteries, the great unknowns that frighten us all.

* * *

We have spent a good portion of our last decades erasing the past. The episode of the gas ovens is closed, wrapped in the mist of history. It is as if it never happened. At the very least, which always surprises me, it is considered a kind of historical novel, abstract and not particularly terrifying.

It is important for children to have books that confront the evils and do not back away from them. Such books can provide a sense of good and evil, a moral reference point. If our fantasy books are not strong enough—and many modern fantasies shy away from asking for sacrifice, preferring to proffer rewards first as if testing the faerie waters—then real stories, like those of Adolf Hitler's evil deeds, will seem like so much slanted news, not to be believed.

Why do so many fantasies shy away from Tough Magic? Why do they offer sweet fairy dances in the moonlight without the fear of the cold dawn that comes after? Because writing about Tough Magic takes courage on the author's part as well. To bring up all the dark, unknown, frightening images that live within each of us and to try to make some sense of them on the page is a task that takes courage indeed. It is not an impersonal courage. Only by taking great risks can the tale succeed. Ursula Le Guin has written: "The artist who goes into himself most deeply—and it is a painful journey—is the artist who touches us most closely, speaks to us most clearly."

Pain and joy are paradoxically two sides of the coin for the artist who, having gone into and touched himself, emerges to carry that flame to the rest of the world.

Prometheus exemplifies the commitment required of the artist. The artist produces flame for others, but by so doing opens up a passage in his own breast. The vultures can reach the heart as easily as the liver. And the artist alone cannot close down the hole again.

Here There Be Dragons

The old sailing charts served both as guides and as warnings. North, south, east, and west were decorated with apple-cheeked winds. Islands, real and imagined, were marked, though the latter had "E. D.," *existence doubtful,* inked in after the names. Here and there were pictures of capering sea nymphs or tritons blowing their conch-shell horns. And somewhere on the map was sure to be the dire sentence: *Here There Be Dragons.*

Did that mean real dragons, with wings and claws and jaws as big as furnaces? Certainly the pictures suggested as much. But sailors brave enough to cross that labeled bit of sea found no such beasts, of course. Instead, they found maelstroms and contrary winds; they found the flotsam and jetsam of past wrecks. It was enough. The dangers were real even if the dragons were not. Map-making was akin to the art of foretelling, and the oracular voice uses the metaphoric mode. Whether one died in the teeth of a dragon or in the teeth of a storm mattered not a whit. One was dead either way.

Here there be dragons. If an effective fantasy story is about any one thing, it is about that. Cross at your peril. There is something awe-ful here.

To a child, the entire world is mapped out that way, filled with prohibitory, metaphoric captions. Don't talk to strangers. Don't cross the street without looking in all directions. Don't forget to eat your green beans. Don't step on the lines. There seems to be no end to dragons, and the only way to conquer them is—to grow up.

Why else is the classic fantasy story a quest tale in which a (usually) small, powerless hero or heroine goes in search of some magical thing and, in the process, grows up? Peter Prescott in *Newsweek* wrote that the hero searches "for competence and wholeness." Isn't that what we mean by being an adult?

In the great fantasy stories it is the same. We meet Ged in *A Wizard of Earthsea* as a boy who at first misuses power and then, in seeking for the released shadow side of his magic, tries to integrate himself. Young Arrietty in *The Borrowers* is both a child and a mannikin no bigger than a thumb. She looks for a safe place to live. The assistant pigkeeper in the Prydain books is made to feel powerless indeed, and he longs to find his father. Hobbits are even smaller than dwarves, yet they must save the world.

And think about the story of King Arthur, the high fantasy, the classic quest. Consider this: the story of Arthur begins with a foster child, orphaned, unsure of his own background and worth. This small, insignificant fosterling actually has an unknown power coursing through his veins—the blood of kings, the lore of magicians. The sword he draws from the stone confers majesty on him, but not adulthood. For the Arthur we all know and love is really a child, not a man, untouched by the sexual passion that ravages his queen. He forgives Guinevere and Lancelot their love because he does not really understand what drives them. Like a child watching a romantic adventure movie, he closes his eyes to the kissing scenes. He concentrates instead on a boy's passions: gathering his best friends together, pushing them on to be honest and true with one another, leading them on forays against evil and wickedness as defined by dragons and giants and black enchanters. Arthur never really grows up, though he grows old. He remains one of our most persistent child-dreams.

Arthur, Ged, Arrietty, Peter Pan. Small, powerless, the child-cipher on a journey toward (though not always achieving) maturity.

And along the way: *Here there be dragons.*

One might call this kind of book a "world" book. There are two reasons for this designation. First, because such a book is creating and opening up a marvelous new world. And second, because the reader's own real world is opened to him or her in the process of exploring the fantasy world of the story.

***

The amazing thing about the fantasy world is its absolute consistency. Within the walls of any given fantasy world, all is logical. Of course, the world may be posited on the most illogical premise *A* (animals can converse with one another, the inhabitants are all a pack of cards), and move from there to equally illogical premise *B*. But the path between *A* and *B* is strictly a logical one. All the rules that have been set down for that world, fantastic as the rules may be, have to work as surely as gravity works on our own world. No one—not the characters or the author—can set those given rules aside.

This lawful universe has led Lloyd Alexander to remark that "the muse of fantasy wears good sensible shoes." One can imagine them as a solid size eight and a half. No golden slipper or glass slingback for Ms. Muse. She had a lot of work to do, making sure the unbelievable is believed, for if the fantasist should falter while providing a logical framework for a story, there is no one who will feel safe in that world. The map must be securely drawn. *Here there be dragons*...and there there be none, for there is nothing more annoying than getting lost in a place you thought you knew well. It is simply not fair.

The most common complaint of childhood is, "It's not fair." And though I have often been heard explaining, "Life is not fair," to a child who thinks he has a smaller piece of pie or notices his bedtime is an hour earlier than his best friend's, in a fantasy book life *has* to be fair. Fair, just, and ordered. And that logically ordered fantasy universe is probably the most important part of a fantasy book.

In order to be believed, the fantasy story must, paradoxically, convince one of its reality. Logic is the key, the map, the template.

Before the days of print, such stories were easier to believe. But words on paper have now accumulated a kind of acquired cynicism. We are not as open to the taradiddle, the fancy, the fantasy. So the writer has first to break down the walls of disbelief. Only belief begets belief. The *author* has to believe in the created world as well as the reader.

The mathematician/biologist J. B. S. Haldane has written, "How do you know that the planet Mars isn't carried around by an angel?" We don't. Not really. But we are conditioned by years of belief to think it is not. Releasing us from that conditioning is what the fantasy writer must strive for. Give me a chance, asks the writer, and I can convince anyone that Mars is really supported by angel arms. And Jupiter as well. Or at least I can convince for the space and time it takes to tell my story.

There are tricks, of course, for inducing that belief. Logical progression is one of them. Another is the overpowering accumulation of facts. If I can show you the dimensions of an angel's arm, the size and shape of angel shoulders, and the overpowering reasons why an angel should want to carry Mars about—then you would be forced by the logic of my reasoning and the power behind my prose to accept it as true, to surrender yourself to my thesis for the space of my book.

Surrender. That is the important word. The author must surrender as well to the logic of the world, to the immutable laws that say that the only way Mars can stay in the part of the sky where our telescopes and probes say it is to be found is by being supported day and night on the back of a seraphic Atlas. And then the reader will see, as does the writer, that the Martian canals are not canals at all but the fiery hair with which the planet is bound to the angel's back. And any haze obscuring the planet is the breath of the angel who tries, periodically, to check the burden he carries. His powerful hands occasionally shift the world from one side of his back to the other, creating vast pressures on the planet's surface, breaking off mountains, forming plateaus. Of course the writer believes it. And so will the reader—for the space and time created by the book.

For that is what a book does, creates its own space and time.

Cover to cover, it defines a world, lays down its own laws, and is then governed by them. A fantasy world is pure speculation, a map of the human psyche labeled north, south, east, west. But it is a true map, nonetheless, and no one knows better than the traveler who uses that particular map whether there really be dragons where X marks the spot.

PART THREE
Wild Child, Feral Child

The Gift of Tongues

In the tenth edition of *Systema Naturae,* published in 1758, the naturalist Linnaeus first introduced the name and concept of feral man. But long before that scientific book, the stories of wild children suckled by animals, grubbing out solitary existences in the woods, subsisting on raw plants or carrion, had a life in the folklore of our planet.

There were Romulus and Remus, nursed by a she-wolf. There was Iamus, fed with honey by two serpents. Ptolemy I, nurtured by an eagle. Lugaid MacCon, kept alive by a dog. Paris and Atalanta, nourished by bears. The stories are so prevalent that they have their own motif number in the mammoth Stith Thompson *Motif Index,* B535. In folkloric terms, for a child to have an animal nurse is a signal that a hero or heroine has been born. Only greatness can come from such beginnings.

These stories have, for many scholars, a substratum of truth. And indeed, life came around again and again to clumsily imitate art. From the nineteenth century on, there have been substantiated reports, complete with photographs and learned depositions, from India, Africa, and elsewhere about the discovery of feral children. Sometimes these prove to be hoaxes or, as in the case of the jungle boy found in 1976 in Burundi, central Africa, a severely retarded child, not a child raised by an animal nurse. But still the reports come in. In the 1850s, a rash of books and pamphlets about the phenomenon culminated in the popular "A Journey to the Kingdom of Oude" by Major General Sir W. H. Sleeman, K. C. B. Published in 1858, it contained a startling account of six wolf children, two of whom Sleeman claimed to have seen personally.

The most famous and completely documented case of a feral child is that of Dr. Jean-Marc Itard's Victor, the wild boy of Aveyron. In 1799, in the autumn and winter of the year, a naked boy was seen swimming, drinking from streams, climbing trees, running on all fours, rooting for bulbs, and baying at the sky. Captured and brought forcibly into civilization, the boy was diagnosed as an "incurable idiot." But he was not. Painstakingly, Itard worked with the wild child trying to teach him language and thus restore him to his human heritage. Itard failed—yet he succeeded in part. Twenty years later, Victor had adopted some of the rudiments of civilization, wearing them as uneasily as a trained animal wears a costume. He could dress himself, eat at a table, be reasonably pleasant to other human beings. But he died with only three words in his spoken vocabulary.

Like Victor, the other authenticated cases of feral humans never really reclaimed their lost humanity. They had in common several problems. In Linnaeus's classification, they were *tetrapus* or four-footed. They habitually walked on hands and feet or hands and knees. They stood upright with difficulty, could remain erect only after long and arduous re-education. However, they were surprisingly fast on four "legs," often outdistancing human runners, though they were never as fast as the animals they followed.

The feral children recovered were also *mutus,* again Linnaeus's term. They had no language, no words other than their animal grunts, barks, howls, or growls. And while author Jean Craighead George, a well-known naturalist, citing the famous Brookfield study of wolves, reports that the animals have "facial expressions, movements, and positions of tails, ears, and head [that] were seen as a language," linguists resist such an appellation. They say, instead, that animal "language" is extremely limited, incapable of growth, while human language is creative and capable of virtually unlimited expansion.

The wild children's inability to speak was not linked to hearing impairment. Indeed, in most cases they had extremely acute hearing. The wolf girls of Midnapore, for example, while turning at sounds and identifying animals by voices, were reported to be mute of human words. The Rev. J. A. L. Singh, who helped capture and retrain them, wrote: "No sound came from their mouths…[only] a peculiar cry or howling in the dead of night." Kamala, after nine years of intensive schooling by the Reverend Singh, had less than a chimpanzee's human-taught vocabulary of fifty words. Kamala could respond to spoken commands, but never initiated conversation. The Cranenberg girl, rescued at eighteen, never learned to speak.

This lack of language has been considered by psychologists and psycholinguists to be the most significant feature of the feral child. *Mutus.*

* * *

That the first years of human life are significant for physical, mental, and emotional development has been known for at least a century. As early as 1885, Rauber pointed this out specifically in connection with feral man. Isolation at an early age can create changes in a human so complete as to make that individual unrecoverable *as a human.* In other words, being human depends on human contact. We are not so much social animals as societal animals. We become human because of our human society.

Dr. Robert Zingg, who studied wild children, wrote succinctly, "Man is born with a neural organization unique in the biological realm, yet apparently the individual has to live with other human beings in order to enter his human heritage." Humanity leans on humanity. For if a human is raised with or by an animal, the human neural equipment becomes conditioned to animal behavior: locomotion, animal responses, food, patterns of sleep. If the animal patterning is too strong or the early human patterning too weak, the result is closer to the beast than to the human. What arises from the jungle floor is no Tarzan/Mowgli superhero but a languageless caricature of a human. Brain-damaged, body-damaged, lacking the behavior patterns of humankind, the feral child can never again be whole.

Two stories from early experiments with language are fascinating. Take them as apocrypha or take them as truth, there is a moral either way.

The Egyptian king Psammetichus believed that if he raised a child who never heard human speech, that child would spontaneously utter words from the world's oldest language. He, of course, believed that tongue to be Egyptian.

So he caused two newborn slave children to be carried away from their mothers and brought up in total verbal isolation. No one who cared for them was ever allowed to speak.

The children grew up, never uttering a sound, until one day, quite by accident, one of them said "Bekos," which is the Phrygian word for bread.

The king reluctantly concluded that the Phrygians, not the Egyptians, were the oldest inhabitants of the earth. Nothing more is reported about the mute slaves.

It was also said that James I of England wanted to try a similar experiment because he believed such children would speak "pure Hebrew." However, since there were no slaves and James was not such an absolute monarch as Psammetichus, the English experiment was never begun.

***

All children are born feral. They are *taught* to be human. When those of us who are outwardly whole meet a child or adult who has been damaged, we are uncomfortable, sensing the path not chosen. We see ourselves caricatured, we see what we *might have* been, had we been less fortunate.

We are drawn to stories in which animal fosterlings are gods not because they are real, but precisely because they are unreal. The stories on the deeper level speak of humanity's climb out of the beast state. And in each tale, it is not the opposable thumb that makes the difference, but the gift of tongues. The hero can speak to animals *and* to humans and so is doubled, is greater than either.

We adore the feral heroes: Romulus, Atalanta, Mowgli, Tarzan. We fear the man-beasts: werewolf, man-eater, *loup-garou.*

"We are, I know not how," writes Montaigne, "double within ourselves." We recognize our dual nature, and fear it. This accounts for the fascination of the stories of feral children. The wild child is the embodiment of a deeply hidden part of our own natures.

The wild child or feral child, lacking language, also lacks true memory, and thus lacks the basis for thought. Helen Keller was lucky—with her fingers in the water, she was reborn. "Everything had a name and each name gave birth to a new thought," she said. Helen Keller, who had been, for a few long years, in a feral state, knew better than anyone the true nature of the beast.

An Inlet for Apple Pie

The gift of words is magic. It can turn a beast into a human as surely as the moon forces the werewolf's change. The loss of words can condemn a human to beast form.

But the gift of words has to be preceded by the capacity to wonder, the result of the human brain and tongue working in conjunction. We are not, after all, mere word machines. Computers may write stories by placing one word in front of another, but the computer cannot judge which is the most interesting tale.

The capacity to wonder, then, is basic. "To be surprised, to wonder," wrote Ortega y Gasset, "is to begin to understand."

When a child is about four years old, he or she is a theologian. "What is God? Where is heaven? Did I love you when I was in your tummy?" The questions come tumbling out. The world is still so new to their eyes and ears, so wonderful and wonder-filled, they hate to go to sleep at night for fear of letting it all go.

Other children may be both less religious and more specific. "What does the wind taste like? Where does the sun go? When is tomorrow?" All children ask variations of those queries. And the Opies write that "A child who does not feel wonder is but an inlet for apple pie."

The early tales and stories from the childhood of the human race came directly from asking questions similar to those that children ask. And all the best answers of the shamans and storytellers and seers were collected in the oral channel and flowed down through the locks of time until they reached print at last. The answers were not straightforward, of course; they were oracular guesses, extended metaphors, which poet John Ciardi has described as "exactly felt errors." Those answers, in turn, led to more stories and more tales. Our history is apocrypha, humanity's innumerable glosses on great unanswerable questions.

What we must never forget, though, is that the answers come from human sources. The storyteller, the writer, is a human mired in society. The writer's art represents the ideas and beliefs and prejudices of a particular society, preserving them like flies in amber. And the power of words in print is far beyond that of the spoken word. The black and white glyphs on a page convey a conviction, a ring of *truth* far greater and more subtle than that which is sent into the air. Every written-down story carries as much binding power as a contract. Speech is ephemeral. It soon fades away. A book remains for the life of its paper and print and thus its imprint persists on the lives of its hundreds, even thousands, of readers.

Gifts do not come free. The price, in this case, is vigilance. We must watch our language, we must preserve our stories, we must guard the magic that is inherent in imagination. The Huns and Vandals are always at the gates. And storytellers must remember that, in the words of the great mage in *A Wizard of Earthsea,* "to light a candle is to cast a shadow."

Knowing that, that magic has consequences, whether it is the magic of wonder, the magic of language, or the magic of challenging a waiting mind, then it is up to the artist, the writer, the storyteller to reach out and touch that awesome magic. Touch magic—and pass it on.

It will be changed by that passage, of course. But so, in the passing, will we. And so, too, will our *listeners,* those who come after.

PART FOUR
Touchstones

Story in Ten Fits

Literature is a textually transmitted disease, normally contracted in childhood. While an occasional reader manages to get through those early years without contact with a book, most of us who are afflicted by *literitis* (that's the medical term) get it early. Its symptoms are an inability to go by a bookstore without stopping in, a passion for late night reading, wrinkled skin from bathtub books, tendonitis from typing, large bottoms from all that sitting, and squinty eyes.

I remember how, as a child, I used to curl up on the window seat of our Manhattan apartment reading volumes like E. Nesbit's *The Phoenix and the Carpet,* Kenneth Grahame's *The Wind in the Willows,* James Thurber's *The Thirteen Clocks,* and every one of Andrew Lang's colored fairy books, while down below on 97th Street and Central Park West the real world went along its way totally unobserved by me.

I remember even earlier riding home with my mother on a bus from the Hampton Roads, Virginia, library with my treasure of five picture books (all they allowed), and reading every single one of them before we got back to Grandma's.

I remember the children's books I read back then more vividly than most of the adult books I have read since. And the difference is that all those children's books were concerned with one thing.

Story.

While books meant for the adult market have gone through years of experimentation with things like minimalism and postmodernism and stream-of-consciousness and even stream-of-unconsciousness; with flash-forwards and flash-backwards and flashes in the pan; with multiple viewpoints and singular viewpoints and no viewpoints at all; children's books still rely on that old standby—story.

In story, there is an unreconstructed beginning, a solid middle, and an ending that wraps up—if not neatly and not always happily—the dangling threads of plot. There are definable and recognizable characters who go forward and do what characters are supposed to do. There is subtext that, like a good solid basement of a house, supports the whole structure, including the chandelier and the cable connections. But first and last and always, there is story because, as Isaac Bashevis Singer said about children when he won the National Book Award, "they love interesting stories, not commentary, guides, or footnotes."

I am not sure that I can tell you precisely what story is. I can, though, in ten fits of literitis, tell you what story is not.

1. *Story is not a moral.* It does not matter if that moral is a home truth learned at mother's knee; or a secular truth learned at school; or a religious truth learned at church or synagogue or under a Bo tree; or a political truth learned by listening to historians or politicians (two very different truths, one might be cynical enough to add). *Moral* has no place in a work of fiction. Dylan Thomas wrote in "Over Sir John's Hill" that we are all "young Aesops fabling to the near night." But Aesop was careful to tell his story first. Please note that Aesop's morals come *after* the story and are not stuck right there in the middle.

In 1968, the *New York Times* reported that the Chinese were recruiting "an army of storytellers" who were ordered to fan out into the countryside and disseminate the thoughts of Chairman Mao. They were to tell all kinds of stories that were supposed to end with "As a result, the evil wind of planting-more-watermelons-for-profit was checked." That's as sorry an excuse for storytelling as I have ever heard, a veritable slough of despond.

Again, the blessed Bashevis Singer wrote, "In art, truth that is boring is not true."

2. *Story is not a history,* even though the word ends in the word "story"—and once upon a time they were pretty interchangeable, the Venerable Bede and the indisputable Josephus knowing a good thing when they got a hold of it.

History is a rough approximation of facts without the sandpaper touch of art. History is reportage, but a story is a promise made between writer and reader. In history you can chart a battle, map the changes in a border, count the gross national product of any one country in any one year. But story has an infinity of borders within the actual outline of its telling. Ask any reader of a story about the parameters of the tale, and the border will exactly match that particular reader's own heart.

History is untidy and we cannot select from it without making hash of the rest. But art, if it is anything, is selective. The writer selects those details that make up the story, chooses the bones and blood and skin. Blows the life into it. And then the blessed thing asks the reader to dance across the pages, history be damned.

3. *Story is not a grammar.* That is, it is not the sum of its gerundive phrases, it is not clause encounters of the third kind. Moliére once wrote that "Grammar...rules even kings." Perhaps Louis XIV was ruled by it. But Charles Perrault was not.

Recently I received a disturbing letter from a child reader. She wrote: "I loved the meddlefurs in your book *Owl Moon.*" Her teacher had used the book as a grammar lesson and destroyed it because story is not a grammar. A reader must "fall through the words into the story," as author Gordon R. Dickson says.

Not grammar, but I will agree that story must be made of *gramarye,* which is *magic* in the old tongue, a word revived by Sir Walter Scott even as he was busy reviving storytelling.

4. *Story is not a compilation, a potpourri, a salad, or a stew.* It will have seasonings, assuredly, and body. It may have any number of

parts. But they all must be kneaded into the whole, like—to stretch this metaphor to the bursting point—a wonderful bread. Or they are layered as neatly as *Sachertorte*. Stews and salads are committee meals. But a story—though it may be protean and full of protein—is simply not created that way.

5. *Story is not a display of wit.* What is dazzling and delicious to your friends in a dinner conversation or in a speech is not what makes a story. While the occasional *bon mot* within the body of a story might make things sparkle, a steady round of them simply gets in the way, as anyone who has read a complete Noel Coward or complete Saki knows. Even Oscar Wilde is boring at length. It is why he wrote so few novels.

6. *Story is not an outpouring of authorial bodily fluids.* As Meredith once said of a competitor, "Poor old James, he sets down on paper these mysterious rumblings in his bowels—but who could be expected to understand them?" English teachers study vowels, doctors study bowels. We should rely on neither for story.

Quite simply, if your spleen needs venting, write a splenetic letter to the editor. If your bowels need moving, there is other paper for that. And if you feel a need to go for the jugular—yours or someone else's—that is why paper towels were invented. One should not have to clean up after a story.

7. *Story is not a showcase for technique.* Barry Moser once told me, speaking of making fine press books, that typography is the invisible art, working best when no one notices it. I think that is true of any kind of authorial technique. The minute one steps back as a reader and says, "Ah, lovely watering on the silk, marvelous duct work, look at that dovetailing, splendid spiral stitching and couching..." we have lost the point of the story. William Morris cautioned craftsmen this way: "It is only the apprentice or a botcher who has to think of the how, or worry about what one calls technique. The master of any trade can keep his eye on the work and what he wants to do, and leave his hand to get it out."

I always figure that a writer who has let us see the technique is either an apprentice—or a botcher. Or somehow *wants* us to think he is.

8. *Story is not a map or a chart,* though certainly place names, landscape, and journey are part of it. E.C. Bentley has quipped, "Geography is about maps, but biography is about chaps." Leaving aside the question of sexism in that couplet, story is about chaps. Story's map is of the human heart.

Just like a map or chart, story has this particular charm: one can travel all over the world without, as Cervantes remarked, "the inconveniences of heat, cold, hunger, and thirst." But a map, no matter how cleverly drawn, is a landscape on a single plane. Story charts more. It dives deeper, climbs higher, tastes the very salt of the briny sea.

***

Now, after eight of my ten fits, you're probably thinking—like the master of the wayside India railway station who sent a message to company headquarters—"Tigress on the line; wire instructions." I have been going on and on, growling about what story is not.

Well, this is simply because it is easier to say what it isn't than what it is. But I can assure you, as someone once defined art, I know it when I see it.

I knew it as a child on that window seat in Manhattan and on that bus, riding home with my treasured books in my lap. I knew it the night of my twelfth birthday when I stayed up all night reading my brand new *Compleat Sherlock Holmes.* I knew it the day I read Doestoevsky's *The Idiot* in my Smith College dorm room as the sun went down and I couldn't even take a moment to turn on the light but kept reading on and on into the deepening gloom. I knew it the day on the ferry from Orkney, reading one of David McKay Brown's book of tales, so entranced that not even the stormy seas could pull me from it.

Jean-Jacques Rousseau knew it when he wrote: "[My father and I] found ourselves so interested in the adventures [the books] contained that we alternately read whole nights together, and could not bear to give over until at the conclusion of the volume. Sometimes in the morning, on hearing the swallows at our window, my father, quite ashamed of this weakness, would cry: 'Come, let us go to bed; I am more a child than thou art.' "

More a child than thou art. There's the secret. Write a story to please that listening child within. The brain is a narrative device that needs stories, indeed.

"Literature," Michael Korda has written, "good, bad, and indifferent, shapes our lives. When we are young, it is the stuff of our dreams, fantasies, ambitions…All the lessons of life are there, buried in great books and great drama." The operative word is, of course, *buried.* And what it is all buried in, is story.

As humans, we are natural storytellers. It is simply what distinguishes us from animals. We define ourselves, our worlds, our lives, by using stories. And this storytelling ability is so familiar to us, we almost forget we have it, every single one of us.

Don't we tell anecdotes about what happened to us during the day? Haven't we all recently given someone a fairly outlandish excuse about being late—to a party, to a meeting, to a class, or to an editor because a manuscript is long overdue? Been to a family gathering recently and reminisced? All story.

Of course, the written-down story differs from these mouth tales because it is more consciously constructed and, once written down and published, rarely changes again.

***

9. *Story is not just an opening.* Because story, like most good things in the universe—the sun, the moon, the eyes of flowers, a young child's face, chocolate chip cookies—are round, a story should be rounded too. We are drawn in by the opening, but we must follow the circle of a story.

10. *Story is not a lie.* Surely what we write down as fiction, by its very nature, is an untruth, a tarradiddle. It is not actual. The act of sub-creation (Tolkien's term) means we build with false blocks. *Writ in water,* as it said on Keats's tomb. This much I will grant.

But what occurs when a story is read is a transformation, a transmutation, a veritable transubstantiation as great as any in magic or religion. What we write is false, yet read, it becomes true.

Perhaps then I *can* give a definition of story. Not only what it is not, but what it is: bread into flesh, wine into blood. A story is made complete by the reader. It is a literary Eucharist.

Go now. The lecture is ended.

Touchstones

Once upon a time…the phrase that places us squarely in the magic realm comes from the original signposts to Faerie, the folktales, or, as the Grimm brothers liked to call them, the *volkseele,* the folk soul. *Once upon a time* is a magical incantation that recalls us to that spot where time is and is not, where as one wag put it, "things never were and always are." The timelessness of the fantasy world begins for all of us with that opening line. We are caught, hooked, turned to stone for the duration of the tale.

And then, to round off the world, there is the traditional fairy tale closing where folk live happily ever after. But not, we must remind ourselves, without careful attention to that first grim taste of hard justice. The wicked queen must dance in red hot shoes until she drops down dead. The bad sister must forever speak mouthfuls of toads. The troll under the bridge must die a horrible death on the great goat's horns. Until these little pieces of frontier justice are meted out, we cannot leave the timeless world, for it is a place where justice is not capricious. It is a land where a hero may die and yet live, and where magic works as surely as gravity does in ours.

Only after we give a nod to the folktales and acknowledge their sure power over us, can we move on to other touchstones. For me these are still the cradle books, nursery fare, and the first stories that engraved their initials on our wondering child hearts; *Peter Rabbit, The Golden Key, The Jungle Books, The Thirteen Clocks,* and *Charlotte's Web* are five that I particularly want to single out.

* * *

When Beatrix Potter wrote and illustrated *Peter Rabbit,* it was as a picture letter to a young friend, Noel Moore, who lay ill in September 1893. That letter was the first of many to the Moore children, and for almost a hundred years *Peter Rabbit* and its successors have introduced children on both sides of the Atlantic to a particular brand of fantasy. Here is the easy transportation between worlds, the real world of Mr. McGregor's garden of carefully cultivated lettuce, radishes, broad beans, and parsley, and the fairy tale world of talking rabbits who wear little blue jackets with brass buttons and drink chamomile tea. The seams of the bridges do not show at all, for Potter has consummate, homey skill. The "tea cosy effect" is in full force here, which means there is plenty of eating being done throughout.

It is in childhood, of course, that we cross and recross the borders between the real and unreal worlds without worrying about passports and visas and custom guards. In fantasy the emphasis is on the worlds themselves, while in science fiction it is the mechanics of the crossing and the amount of customs to be paid that counts. We can see these same comfortable crossings in the great childhood fantasy novels of C.S. Lewis and E. Nesbit and Kenneth Grahame and, later on, in the animal fantasies like *Watership Down, Animal Farm, Abel's Island, The Book of the Dun Cow.*

George MacDonald was a Scottish visionary minister who turned to writing when his offended parishioners revolted against his unorthodox religious ideas and kicked him from the church. The pulpit's loss was literature's gain, and story followed story, novel followed novel, as well as plays, literary criticism, poetry, and translations. The main body of MacDonald's work was written and published in the late nineteenth and early twentieth centuries. His books are stories with an emphasis on the allegorical and the archetypal, with—as one critic put it—"some peculiar and suggestive symbolism." He was also steeped in the Victorian attitude regarding children as both innocent and wise. These archetypes and symbols and the attitude that couples wisdom and naiveté can be encountered in MacDonald's *The Light Princess, At the Back of the North Wind, The Princess and the Goblin,* some of his more famous pieces for children. But to my mind, the most beautiful of all is *The Golden Key.* MacDonald's stories prefigured the work of such fantasy authors as Patricia McKillip and Lloyd Alexander and, to some extent, my own fairy tales. One particular passage in *The Golden Key,* where the old man of the earth urges the children to throw themselves into the great gaping hole before them, has always seemed to be a metaphor for fantasy itself.

> The Old Man of the Earth stooped over the floor of the cave, raised a huge stone from it, and left it leaning. It disclosed a great hole that went plumb-down.
> "That is the way," he said.
> "But there are no stairs."
> "You must throw yourself in. There is no other way."

To enjoy fantasy, one must throw oneself in for, indeed, there is no other way to enter Faerie.

***

The India that Rudyard Kipling writes about in his enduring *The Jungle Books* is as magical a place as any totally fantasy realm. Written as the nineteenth century closed, when Kipling was living with his young family in Vermont, *The Jungle Books* is the story of the feral child Mowgli and his animal brothers and sisters. It is a perfect metaphor for human society as Kipling viewed it. Always feeling the outsider, he made his greatest hero the ultimate outsider, a being between two societies, longing for both and not wholly in either—a human among animals, an animal among humans. This story-as-societal-metaphor would come to fruition later in the worlds of Ursula Le Guin where, like Kipling, the language is elevated, alternately sonorous and somber, and filled with light. The mood of *The Jungle Books* is heroic throughout. After Kipling would come Burroughs' Tarzan, of course, and all the wonderful heroics of

Andre Norton. For me, Kipling is at his best in this passage—where sentiment and sentimentality meet in a heroic death—from near the end of "Red Dog," the chapter in *The Jungle Books* where Akela, the leader of the wolves and Mowgli's adopted father, dies.

> Very carefully and gently Mowgli raised Akela to his feet, both arms around him, and the Lone Wolf drew a deep Breath and began the Death Song that a leader of the pack should sing when he dies. It gathered strength as he went on, lifting and lifting and ringing far and across the river, till it came to the last "Good hunting" and Akela shook himself clear of Mowgli for an instant, and leaping into the air, fell backwards dead upon his last and most terrible kill.
>
> Mowgli sat with his head on his knees, careless of anything else, while the last of the dying dholes were being overtaken and run down by the merciless *labinis*. Little by little the cries died away and the wolves came back limping as if their wounds stiffened to take stock of the dead. Fifteen of the pack, as well as half a dozen *labinis*, were dead by the river, and of the others not one was unmarked. Mowgli sat through it all through the cold daybreak, when Phao's wet red muzzle was dropped in his hand, and Mowgli drew back to show the gaunt body of Akela.
>
> "Good Hunting," said Phao, as though Akela were still alive, and then over his bitten shoulder to the others: "Howl, dogs. A wolf has died tonight."

* * *

Whimsy is surely a part of fantasy as well as somber heroics, though the two rarely meet in a single book. No one, not even A.A. Milne, does whimsy better than James Thurber, who always mixed a little bit of acid in his ink. Thurber, that consummate New *Yorker* writer and cartoonist, penned some of the slyest and wittiest books for children that can be enjoyed (and quoted) by adults. *Many Moons* won a Caldecott medal for its pictures, though its charming, upbeat story is where the real interest lies. *The White Deer, The Wonderful O,* and *The Great Quillow,* his other books for young readers, have considerable charm and delight. But to my mind, his most endearing and enduring is *The Thirteen Clocks,* written in 1950 and called by Thurber "an example of escapism and self-indulgence" in a foreword to the book. Part fairy tale, part madcap misdirection, *The Thirteen Clocks* is full of clichés stood upon their heads, and delightful sentences that seem much simpler than they actually are: "The cold Duke was afraid of Now, for Now has warmth and urgency, and Then is dead and buried." "We all have flaws," he said, "and mine is being wicked." And Thurber, in his inimitably droll fashion created phrases that made their way into the national consciousness as well: "slit him from his guggle to his zatch." Thurber does in print what Danny Kaye, in his best movies ("The Court Jester" for example), does on the screen: forces us to look again and laugh again and love again all the old fairy tale conventions. Peter Beagle's *The Last Unicorn* might be considered a follow-up, and so might Jonathan Carroll's *The Land of Laughs.*

***

The quintessential American writer, E.B. White, another *New Yorker* staff writer, authored only three children's books but he brought to his fantasy stories—*Stuart Little, The Trumpet of the Swan,* and most especially *Charlotte's Web*—the realist's eye. White had such a clear way of writing, a precision, an exactly held vision, that he made what was unreal (the story of a slightly whiny, self-involved pig and his best friend, a noble spider) entirely imaginable. No details of the barn or the fair or the yard were imprecise or fuzzy. It was all so true that it also had to be True.

> The barn was very large. It was very old. It smelled of hay and it smelled of manure. It smelled of the perspiration of tired horses and the wonderful sweet breath of patient cows. It often had a sort of peaceful smell—as though nothing bad could happen ever again in the world. It smelled of grain and of harness dressing and of axle grease and of rubber boots and of new rope. And whenever the cat was given a new fish-head to eat, the barn would smell of fish. But mostly it smelled of hay, for there was always hay in the great loft up overhead. And there was always hay being pitched down to the cows and the horses and the sheep.

The reader believes because White would have it no other way. That delicate balance of detail and mood—creating what Eleanor Cameron, in her magnificent book on fantasy, *The Green and Burning Tree,* calls "the compelling power of place"—was realized wonderfully in White's work. Writers coming after White and trying to mine that same kind of story—where real and unreal are but a barn corner's turn away—would do well to read his lucid, simple, yet fully realized descriptions, and understand the power of a single syllable word.

* * *

These five books are to me true touchstones of fantasy writing, books that are both simple and complex, that are metaphors for the real world, where the real and unreal are layered on one another, a literary Sachertorte.

Fabling to the Near Night

Children know themselves to be the single most powerless unit in today's world. They cannot support themselves, they cannot vote, they have little physical strength, they have but a small knowledge of the universe. They cannot see over walls. As infants they are entirely dependent upon the kindness of adults, and as they grow up further, they are still small satellites in an adult world. They dream of being big enough and old enough and able enough to tame the Wild Things.

In reality, those Wild Things could well devour them.

Therefore, we give them many tools with which to keep the real world at bay until they are ready for it. We give them teachers, we give them toys, we give them chants and prayers and cultural attitudes, and surround them with tribes and tribal constraints.

We give them stories.

The stories we give our children are, in some ways, the most important pieces in the ethical and moral puzzle they are asked to solve from birth on. Do all children's stories teach a moral? Certainly a storyteller's moral sense will *inform* a story. A writer will not choose to tell a story that makes the author uncomfortable at the core. And the reader's moral sense will allow him or her to pick out what he or she needs in the story. But remember Isaac Bashevis Singer's "In art, truth that is boring is not true." The morals—or ethical bones of each tale—are often well hidden beneath the ample flesh.

But make no mistake. As pieces of cultural baggage, these stories are not only not entirely free of ideological viewpoints, they are, in fact, totally encumbered by them.

A story, written (or rewritten) by an individual author, is as mired as its author in a particular time and place. Frederic Jameson has said, "Genres are essentially literary *institutions,* or social contracts between writer and a specific public."

Even fairy tales—which are often claimed to be universal and ageless—carry the thumbprints of their history. A social scientist or international lawyer could parse (as happened at a fairy tale conference I attended) the fairy tale punishments in classic European fairy tales and explain them in terms of the community and era in which each story was told. Thus the witch shoved into the oven in Hansel and Gretel, and the wicked queen in her red hot iron shoes are reflections of the prevailing laws about the burning of witches, and so forth.

That we are mirrors of our time, reflecting prevalent prejudices and class hatreds does not surprise any of us. Recent events—the OJ case, the Kosovar conflict, the killings of children by children in Littleton and elsewhere, tribal genocides in Africa, the ongoing sniping in Israel and Ireland—all these are relevant to any discussion of moral issues. Yet when the author of a fantasy story creates a dark mirror, giving back in its fantastic setting the baser beliefs and feelings and legalities of his own day, it often comes as a shock to the more perspicacious reader (and as a total mystery to those readers who skim along the tops of metaphors.)

Fantasy tales are as much *of* their time as *beyond* it.

Some examples of this are a few children's books with which most readers will be familiar.

Charles Kingsley's *The Water Babies: A Fairy Tale for a Land Baby* (the unexpurgated version, which is—admittedly—difficult to find nowadays) is one such book. Kingsley was a nineteenth-century

Anglican minister who was a founding member of the Christian socialists, which should have made him a liberal in his day. But he was also an avowed anti-Catholic, anti-ascetic, anti-Irish, anti-black, and anti-semite, all of which attitudes found their way into *The Water Babies*.

Kingsley was not a bad man; in fact, he was simply mirroring those particular virulent strains of Victorian prejudice, which manifested itself in laws against the Irish and Jews, as well as attitudes expressed by such worthies as Engels who wrote that the Irish were "slovenly intruders upon the green and pleasant land" of England.

By the time Kingsley wrote *The Water Babies,* he had already penned a number of specifically anti-Catholic tracts and novels. While the references to blacks and Jews are few (but nasty) in *Water Babies,* it is to the Catholic Irish that Kingsley gives full vent to his spleen. The story is about a young chimneysweep who is literally and figuratively wiped clean by the waters of the world and, after a highly symbolic trip to the Other-End-of Nowhere, is reborn.

That Kingsley meant this children's fantasy novel to have political repercussions in his day there is no doubt. He was in the forefront of the movement to help clean up or abolish child labor, and in places the book reads very much like a tract. But for all its concern with the social questions of the day, for all its protestations of social reform, the novel is full of open caricatures and calumnies about the Irish.

Kingsley intimates that the Irish are full of blarney and bluster; that they are naturally lazy and childlike; that they are quarrelsome, querulous, wild; that they are cowardly and coarse. For example, he writes: "And then Dennis will look up at you with his handsome, sly, soft, sleepy, good-natured, untrustable Irish grey eyes, and answer with the prettiest smile, 'Sure, and didn't I think your honour would like a pleasant answer…You must not trust Dennis because he is in the habit of giving pleasant answers; but instead of being angry with him, you must remember that he is a poor Paddy and knows no better.' " If this does not offend you, if this does not set off alarms, remember that the Irish were considered the "niggers" of Victorian England.

***

Moving ahead a number of years, we come to the original *Mary Poppins*. P. L. (Pamela) Travers, an Australian writer living in England, created in her children's books a magical nanny with a turned-up nose, a chimneysweep friend, and an ability to lead four proper English children across the borders of time and space.

In many ways, Mary Poppins is a brilliant conception, years ahead of her time. But on one such trip, the Banks children go with Mary Poppins to the four compass points and in so doing meet black children—she calls them pickaninnies—and little Eskimo children. It is a trip that Travers clearly thought taught the Banks children (and the readers) that all over the world there were children with feelings just like theirs.

In fact, the book underlines the attitude that to be English is to be better than everyone else, an attitude that has changed little since. (Though you must know that I live part time in Scotland and so can be considered prejudiced against the English on such matters.)

Published in 1934, *Mary Poppins* is the first in a series about the magical nanny. Author Pamela Travers had loved fairy tales from childhood on. As an adult she was instrumental in starting the magazine *Parabola,* which deals with myth and folklore. Yet *Mary Poppins,* for all the fairy tales that inform it, was the product of a rather culturally closed author.

Mavis Wormley Davis, writing in *School Library Journal,* remarked, "One of the most startlingly offensive classics is the ever-popular *Mary Poppins. . ."* She points especially to the trip sequence in chapter six where the children encounter

> a man and woman quite black all over with very few clothes on...[with beads] in their ears and one or two in their noses. On the knee of the negro lady sat a tiny black pickaninny with nothing on at all. It smiled at the children as its mother spoke: "Ah bin 'specting you a long time Mar Poppins...You bring dem chillun dere into ma l'il house for a slice of watermelon right now. My, but dem's very white babies. You wan use a lil bit black boot polish on dem."

Ms. Davis writes passionately that "Cordial as she was, the black scantily-clad mother remains an objectionable stereotype, the perennial water-melon fancier, bead-bedecked and uttering the deepest dialect." Remember that neither the dialect nor the water-melon were native to that compass point!

When interviewed about that passage, Travers admitted knowing nothing about Africans. The offending passage was eventually revised because of how much it troubled black readers. The wording was changed but for a long time the illustrations remained the same. And the underlying attitude has never varied.

***

Another author forced by changing attitudes to rework published material was Roald Dahl. In *Charlie and the Chocolate Factory,* the original Oompa-Loompahs were little chocolate-colored pygmies who had been discovered in darkest Africa, and who now play their banjos by the side of the chocolate river in Willa Wonka's factory. There they are used by Wonka in a variety of experiments. But—my! are they happy.

I was a junior editor at Knopf in the early '60s, working on the manuscript of *Charlie and the Chocolate Factory,* having held my job there for less than a month. Dahl was asked by the editor-in-chief to make the Oompa-Loompahs some color other than black, and to drop the references to playing the banjos by the side of the river. But Dahl replied, "Racism is an American problem," and insisted the manuscript not be changed.

Years later, when racism was also a British problem, Dahl bowed to pressure and changed the Oompa-Loompahs to tiny green-skinned people, shifting their place of origin to a South Sea island. This only slightly mitigated the problem of a different-skinned people being held in semi-benign captivity for the reward of food and a place to live.

***

If we fast forward a decade or two, we come to Richard Adams' rabbits in *Watership Down* who—while they can sing and talk and plot and tell stories and make myths, cannot redeem their women-folk from the narrow role of breeders.

99

The first few books of the Brian Jacques *Redwall* series were fast heading for that same slough, till his editor alerted him in time, and his female hero Mariel entered the fray.

And British author Lynn Reid Banks has had endless go-rounds with Native American critics for her ever-popular *Indian in the Cupboard* series, none of whom have been mollified by her repeated reminders that the Indian is only a toy Indian after all.

Northrop Frye has written in *Anatomy of Criticism* that "The corruption out of which human art has been constructed will always remain in the art, but the imaginative quality of the art preserve it in its corruption, like the corpse of a saint."

The problem is, of course, that literature for children will always have a didactic power. The hidden messages can sometimes be the more potent for being hidden.

How hidden are they?

Let me tell you a story.

When I first discovered the magic dispensed by the strange sand fairy, with the gift for wishes, the psammead, in E. Nesbit's *The Story of the Amulet,* I was about seven or eight years old. It was 1946, and I read my magic books eagerly, hungrily, sitting on the window seat in our New York apartment. I hardly heard the noise of the city as the traffic on Central Park West squealed and honked four floors below me. Once into a book, I could leave those mundane sounds behind. An onlooker would have seen a small, dark haired, pigtailed child with a serious, questing face, hunched over a book. But that was not really me. I was already in Neverland, in Wonderland, in Oz.

Or in England.

England was as rich and magical a place to me as any fantasy world. It was the place of Arthur and Merlin and Robin Hood. It was where Ratty and Mole messed about in boats, and from whose shores young Jim Hawkins shipped aboard the *Hispanola* to seek treasure. It was still a place of kings and queens and princesses, which meant to a child my age that it was a land where wizardry must still work and spells must still be spoken.

As a child, I read Nesbit's books uncritically. Her sensible

100

approach to magic, the cozy way she addressed the reader, the very Britishness of the things she wrote about—tea and nannies and school uniforms and such—drew me in.

As I got older and re-read the psammead books while researching Nesbit's life for an article, two things stuck out as never before. First, having learned about Nesbit's unconventional household and her connection with the Fabian socialists and H.G. Wells, I was able to "catch" certain references for the first time, things that had slipped over my head when I was a child reader, such as the little boy named Wells who lives in the future! But I also began to understand that Nesbit—like all authors—was mired in her society with its attendant hatreds and prejudices and misunderstandings. In the Victorian and Edwardian England that I loved so much, knee-jerk anti-semitism was a given in the middle and upper classes.

Now to make this clear: I first read Nesbit's books at the end of the 1940s. I was a young Jewish girl living in New York City. My father had been in the war where he had been wounded by the buzz bombs in London. This was a war fought against the greatest anti-semite of all times.

One could not be a child of that era—especially a Jewish child in New York City—and be unaware of Hitler, the Nazis, the concentration camps, and the appalling arithmetic of the war.

Yet I loved the Nesbit books uncritically, had not ever noticed the small knee-jerk prejudicial parts. I had read past the metaphors, skimming over the things I did not understand, and around the ugly stuff. I had not noticed that Nesbit's characters—like Nesbit herself—were anti what I was. Because when I was in Nesbit's books, I was not me, I was one of them.

I was one of them.

Surely one of the great things about fantasy literature is that we can be transported to worlds we do not know. We can wear skins that are not ours. We can look at the landscape through someone else's eyes.

But what if instead—or indeed, at the same time—we take on someone else's prejudices and hatreds? What if we cheer when all those naughty children get summarily dispatched in the chocolate factory? Or wish that we, too, had a bunch of little chocolate (or perhaps green) skinned workers in our own factories willing to work for candy pay?

***

Does this mean that I advocate building uncritical readers? That we should count on the natural innocence and un-knowingness of children to get them past the real messages in books to the messages we would like them to get?

Or does it mean that I think we must despoil beloved texts so that we do not otherwise have to freight young readers with too much knowledge? That we encourage rewriting those passages in texts to reflect our modern ethics?

Am I recommending censorship? Is this book battery? Is it an assault on literature?

And anyway, whose ethics should we be setting forth?

Should reading be seen as a political act? Or a socializing act? Or is it just plain entertainment?

As a passionate writer—as well as a passionate reader—I decry censorship from the right or the left. As a writer of a great deal of fantasy, I have felt the full brunt of fundamentalist ire. I have been called a "tool of Satan" from the pulpit for my fairy tales. I have had my books hidden behind shelves and stolen from shelves. My book *Briar Rose* was burned on the steps of the Kansas City Board of Education.

Book banning is not what I am advocating.

What I am asking is that we be aware. Aware of what we consider morality, and what we consider ethical behavior. And aware also that this is a sliding scale. I am certain E. Nesbit considered herself a moral person. And Charles Kingsley. And P.L. Travers. And certainly Roald Dahl did, whose morality extended to a letter to the *London Times* saying that he thought Salman Rushdie should, indeed, be shot by his own people for writing against his religion.

But we also must be aware that there is more in our fantasy books than mere story. Every tale carries with it both hidden and open messages.

In *Fairy Tales & the Art of Subversion,* Jack Zipes writes: "The best fairy tales are supposedly universal. It does not matter when or why they were written."

But watch that *supposedly*. Zipes uses it cleverly, provocatively, purposefully. He suggests that art is never free of its cultural and historical references. It is never clean. It is never pure.

The ethical and moral considerations in a story come from a particular time in the author's life. It is a small place bound about with the constraints of *that* very age and *that* very place.

We do not make history so much as we are made by it. And our stories reflect us as much as they re-create in our children's lives all that we think and believe in...now.

This moment.

This pinprick of light on the page.

Killing the Other

For years I have quoted Chesterton's contention that the core of ethics is the core of the nursery tale. Said it—and meant it. I do so in the opening essays of this book.

But as I started to think more carefully about a number of popular folk stories for some other project, I had to revise my long-held opinion, for many of those tales had—at the very least—puzzling moralities.

So, I have to remind myself that even folk tales do not come value free. There is no hall pass in literature.

We are all skim readers first, relying on the high points of plot to carry us along. Only later do we learn to savor munchy language, characterization, the lyrical delineation of place and time. Even later still do we come to appreciate irony, angularity, innovation, and the unreliability of certain narrators.

But how could I have so missed the deep immorality of certain tales while claiming with Chesterton that the fairy stories our mothers and grandmothers told us were chockablock with moral certainty?

Easy.

I read only for story.

I walked the mountain peaks, my eyes on the clouds, not looking at what lay below.

Like most readers, I was a surface feeder.

So here are three of those stories and my musings on them.

***

Puss in Boots.

If one thinks about that inherited cat as a kind of musketeer (or mouseketeer) then the murky morals of the story come clearer. The famous Doré illustrations for the story give a hint of where to start, with the cat dressed in a plumed hat and period boots. He has a sly, contented look on his face. The very model of a feline Athos. Or Porthos. Or Aramis. Recalling what I remembered of the Musketeers, who were allowed to cheat, kill, destroy for their mistress, the queen, I saw how Puss had been made in their image.

In Puss we have a servant who steals, lies, and then murders for his master without a single qualm. The audience is lulled into accepting such bad behavior because—we are told—the one upon whom such depravities are visited is *only* an ogre. And ogres, after all, do not deserve our pity. If in the short space of the tale, the ogre loses his title, his land, and finally his life, we are not to carp. He is, you see, an ogre in a non-ogre world and as such is dispensable.

Substitute the word "Albanian" for ogre, and make the young master a Serb.

Or call them black man, white man.

Or Jew, Nazi.

Or Hutu, Tutsi.

Do I bring PC sensibilities into a fairy tale? Think before knee-jerking that response. Nowhere in the body of the story are we told that the ogre has done anything bad. He has not destroyed villages or raped maidens or pillaged farms. He has taken no prisoners, eaten no cattle. What he has done, though, is the unforgivable. He owns a large property and a title while remaining undeniably an ogre.

In other words, the ogre is the ultimate outsider and therefore it is not only all right to take all that he owns and then kill him, it is virtually incumbent upon Puss to do so. It is heroic action within the murky morality of the tale.

***

Similarly *Rumplestiltskin*.

The eponymous character is the consummate outsider—literally he lives outside of the regular towns. He is not even known to those who live inside. Messengers, spies have to track him down.

But wait. . .let's not get ahead of ourselves. Start from the beginning to find the moral center of the story.

Here is a miller who tells a lie.

His daughter who is complicitous in the lie.

The king who accepts the lie at face value. Why? Because his only motivation in the story is that he wants more gold. If he does not get what he is promised, he will execute both the miller and his daughter.

Are these admirable characters? Are they moral or corrupt? Do we want children to emulate their behavior? Certainly not unimportant questions if this is a nursery tale.

Then consider the following:

Only one character refuses to lie.

Only one character helps out the poor, benighted girl.

Only one character does exactly what he says he will do.

Rumplestiltskin. The Outsider.

Perhaps—as we did with the musketeer Puss in Boots—if we put the story in some sort of quasi-historical context, the problem becomes clearer.

As Rumplestiltskin is a Grimm's tale, let us think about sixteenth- to eighteenth-century Germany.

The story is about a little man with an unpronounceable name, who lives outside the walls of the community, and who is a changer of straw into gold. He wants the child for—the reader presumes— some unspeakable blood ritual.

It doesn't take a very great leap to remember that Jews were ghettoed away from the larger German cities, had different and odd names, were caricatured as a small people, and were allowed by law only to be money changers. Often they were accused of stealing Christian babies for some unnamed blood rites.

(As an aside, the British version, *Tom Tit Tot*, stars a little black imp in the Rumplestiltskin role. And there is another version in which the Outsider character is a Gypsy.)

So the moral of this story is, again, death to the outsider. The underlying theme seems to be that it is alright to renege on promises to an outsider who, by virtue of being an outsider, is obviously up to no good.

***

Finally, let's look at that perennial favorite, *Rapunzel*.

A girl, a tower, a prince—and a witch. A witch that Sheldon Cashdan, in his perceptively titled book, *The Witch Must Die*, notes must be summarily dealt with by the end of the story.

But why? What has the witch in the story done other than take in an unwanted child (her mother trades her for a bowl of onions!) and raise her devotedly.

In effect the witch is a stepmother. But she is also a foster mother, an adoptive mother. Read in one way, the witch is admirable.

When she locks up the adolescent Rapunzel she is doing, metaphorically, what we all do, with curfews and rules about who our daughters can and cannot see.

So what does Rapunzel do? She invites up to her bedroom the very first young man she ever sets eyes on—and gets pregnant. The morals of this story are wobbly at best and go downhill from there.

In the end, the old woman is left alone, after having spent much of her life raising the girl. She never gets to see her step-grandchildren, and the prince (rather latterly) marries the girl he has so severely compromised. My guess is that if he hadn't been injured in the fall, he'd have been on to the next more promising princess in a tower.

***

Again, what I am suggesting is not to ban or censor the stories. They are great and important parts of the Western folk canon.

But what I *am* asking for is that we become better readers. That we read below the surface. That we teach our children to think about what Puss does for his master, why Rumplestiltskin is destroyed, how Rapunzel treats her mother-substitute. I want our children to wonder about Goldilocks' casual destruction of the

Bears' lovely cottage and talk about whether the princess deserves to marry the frog-prince and to figure out what Cinderella's father was doing all the while his new wife and step-daughters are mistreating her.

There are many layers inside the old tales, like nesting Matrushka dolls. Examining the layers does not wreck the story, but shows us how rich and fascinating they really are.

An Experiential Act

Scratch any science fiction or fantasy writer and the red wound of argument appears: science fiction is the subgenre of fantasy or fantasy is the subgenre of science fiction. It is an old fight. However, there is one kind of writing in which the two are so intermingled, it is hard to know which is which, and that is the time travel story.

Essentially there are two kinds of time travel—into the future or into the past. Sometimes the viewpoint character does the traveling: back to King Arthur's court, back to the Children's Crusade, forward to converse with the Eloi. Occasionally it is another character who comes forward or back in time to interact with the main players: Mayne's drummer boy in *Earthfasts,* the child Hatty in *Tom's Midnight Garden,* or Nesbit's psammead.

The implements of travel—those things which allow the traveler to slip through the streams of time like a minnow in a brook—are many. There is Taliesin's tuning fork in Nancy Bond's *A String in the Harp;* there are elaborate devices in H.G. Wells' *Time Machine* and in *Crusade in Jeans.* There are silver pins, magic mirrors, wardrobe cupboards, and conjunctions of moons, planets, stars. In my book, *The Devil's Arithmetic,* a young Jewish girl of the 1980s opens the door for Elijah at the family seder and finds herself back on a shtetl on the Polish-German border in 1942. She is propelled back, into a past that she has been steadfastly refusing to remember, by three things: the great emotional neediness of the Holocaust survivors in her family, the open seder door, and the familiar childhood chant "Ready or not, here I come."

None of us is really ready for a trip into the past or into the future. We all fight time. Children, eager and fearful at once, want to grow up and yet remain young. *Peter Pan* is a perceptive book.

Patricia MacLachlan told me a very poignant story about her oldest son John going out on his very first date to a prom. The entire family had been excited, but Patty found herself getting more and more depressed as the evening progressed. Her little boy was growing up. When he got home, she fought the temptation to quiz him on it. But the next morning, when she came downstairs, a bit nervous and sensitive about what to say, she heard a strange noise. There, on the living room floor, was John with his younger brother and sister, toy car in hand. The noise Patty had heard was John going "Vrrrrrrrooom, vrrrrrrooommm." Boy and man at once.

Children, especially at the time they are reading time travel novels, are a little like Walter de la Mare's "Poor Jim Jay" who

Got stuck fast
In yesterday…
Round veered the weathercock,
The sun drew in—
And stuck was Jim
Like a rusty pin…
But all in vain.
The clock struck one
And there was Jim
A little bit gone…

That is the child at the instant of reading the time travel novel, "a little bit gone." One foot in today and the rest stuck back in 1942 or 1857 or 1066. And though I have heard from at least one editor who feels time travel to be "a gimmick, a device, a framework" only, I believe it is a straight road into memory, an experiential act for an understanding of the past. It is once-upon-a-very-real-time, making history immediate and accessible for the young reader, letting them see backwards through a clear lens.

Is it easier for a child caught between youth and adulthood to believe in layers of time that can be crossed or swum through or peeled away? Certainly it is easier than the simple memorization of rote fact. A ghost recalling its personal history is more exciting than a high school history teacher at the blackboard, chalk squeaking out a variety of forgettable dates. Kipling's Pook's Hill, where history is pressed together like the flowers between a book's pages, is more accessible than a text on British monarchies. And a boy in blue jeans, by asking his newfound friends why they are going on a crusade across thousands of miles, voices the questions any sensible modern child would ask. The answers he receives are more palatable in a friend's mouth than the dry rota of a history professor.

Making history come alive is certainly one of the things that a time travel book can do. But so—one might comfortably argue— could a well-written textbook or historical novel. My counter to that is that children, while natural believers, are also natural cynics. *They know what they know.*

They will not easily believe, for example, that an intelligent person "knew" the world was flat. Maybe a little sister or brother not yet in nursery school, but not a grownup capable of ruling a kingdom or running a ship. So much for Queen Isabella and many of the good sailors of Columbus's time.

They know what they know. They will not easily believe that parents would allow their children to go on a hazardous journey across the Alps with only the company of other children. Not when they have trouble getting permission themselves to stay out an extra half hour on Saturday night. Not when Mom still packs a special bag for their overnight camping trips and Dad does a surreptitious drive-by around ten o'clock at night. So much for the Children's Crusade.

They know what they know. They cannot believe that real people killed men, women, and children in a programmed and mechanical way, stripping their teeth for gold, using their hair to stuff mattresses, boiling down the body fat for soap, using their skin for lampshades, just because they were ordered to do so. This is not, after all, *Friday the 13th, part 27,* with catsup for blood and rubber prostheses. Eighth graders in a well-regarded midwestern private school asked me, horrified, if I had made that stuff up. It was a joke, right? It wasn't real. Not in this century anyway. So much for the concentration camps.

They know what they know.

But take a book that starts in the real world and thrust a young reader back into the heart and mind of someone his or her own age forty or one hundred or a thousand years ago. Let that protagonist ask the questions our young people all want to ask: how can you believe the world is flat when it isn't? How can you trust that the people helping you over the mountains will not enslave you? How can you believe these Nazis when they say you are only being resettled? Because I, the protagonist (and therefore I, the child reader), am from the future and I know better.

The answers they get from the folk in the story will astound them, shake them into new awarenesses, really let them remember and be part of history. Not just "I remembered for the test" but "I know because *I was there.*"

Rosemary Sutcliffe has written about her own reading of Kipling's *Puck of Pook's Hill* that it "linked the past of one corner of England with the present..." so that the child she was, was made to feel it as a living and continuous process of which she was part.

"A living and continuous process." If time travel novels can be said to do any one thing, that is it: they take the past and make it a *living and continuous process* for the child. Children are mired in the present. They cannot see two weeks ahead in order to write their term paper early. They cannot see one year ahead in order to make realistic plans. If they are miserable today, they expect they will be miserable always. If they are happily content, they cannot believe in the possibility that such contentment should ever pass away. It is not death or poverty or fear that surprises them. It is tomorrow.

By taking a child protagonist out of that *today* in a novel, a character that the reader identifies fully with, and throwing the child backward or forward in time, the reader too is thrown into the slipstream of yesterday or tomorrow. The reader becomes a part of that "living and continuous process," forced to acknowledge that we *are* our past just as we *are* our future.

I believe this so strongly that when I was at last ready to confront what—for any Jewish author—has to be the most difficult and unrelieved period in history, the Holocaust, I knew that the only way I could write it was as a time travel novel. I am not sure I thought things through in logical steps. However, it came to me that it was the only way *I* could deal with the story I had to tell.

I wanted my readers to be unable to say, as the Indianapolis eighth graders had said, "Did you make this stuff up?" I wanted to throw them body and soul into that cauldron so that they would understand that it had been all but impossible to fight, except to fight to stay alive. That within that hideous arena there existed not only hate but love, not only carelessness but caring, not only hopelessness but hope, and an abiding truth within the careful catalogues of lies. I wanted my readers to remember as if they had been there, without having to come back to the 1980s with the long numbers scorched into their arms. I wanted them to remember. To witness.

The young protagonist I used as the reader's eyes and ears was myself, the child I had been: a little bit whiny, slightly uncomfortable in her own skin, able to make up stories on the spot, better with younger children than with girls her own age, often impatient, courageous without thinking, though thought makes her afraid. A child who talks more than she thinks, who thinks more than she acts, but when she finally acts, is willing to go through with the action no matter the consequences. I called her Hannah in America, but in the shtetl she is known as Chaya, my daughter's Hebrew name, a name which means *life*.

Hannah is the one who, when the wedding party going through the forest from one village to another comes upon truckloads of soldiers, shouts "They're Nazis. Nazis! Do you understand? They kill people They killed…kill…will kill Jews. Hundreds of them. Thousands of them. Six million of them. I know. Don't ask me how I know. I just do. We have to turn the wagons around. We have to run." Just as any sensible child of today would say who knows a bit

115

of history, who has seen *Schindler's List* or any one of the many adventure stories starring Lee Marvin or Richard Burton kicking around the incompetent SS.

What Hannah doesn't know, what the child reader doesn't know, is the reason why no one will take her advice. After all, the Jews didn't escape the Holocaust. And that is the answer that the rabbi, father of the bride, who wants to comfort a hysterical child, gives her.

> "There are not six million Jews in all Poland, my child. And as for running—where would we run to? God is everywhere. There will always be Nazis among us. No, my child, do not tremble before mere men. It is God before whom we must tremble. Only God. We will go ahead, just as we planned. After all, this is our shtetl, not theirs. And there is still a wedding to be made."

He lifts his hand and on his signal the wagons start across the village marketplace towards the synagogue where the Nazis are waiting for them.

The lesson of history as we learn it in school is clear: the Jews did not run, the children of the crusades marched across the Alps into slavery, Columbus did not fall over the edge of his pride. We cannot change the past. But what few textbooks and history teachers can convince children of is why these people fell into pits, into prisons, into ambushes, into traps. We may look back across our history books and shake our heads wisely, saying they *shouldn't* have. But, in fact, they did. We, in our turn, will do the same.

A living and continuous process. I hope the readers of *The Devil's Arithmetic* feel that. We say, a few decades later, "Never again," yet it is happening again around the world: in Cambodia, in South America, in South Africa, in Afghanistan, in Israel, in Ethiopia, on our own American city streets. Little pieces of the same kind of history with different characters and different names, but recognizable all the same.

Hannah tells her best friend, Rifka, when they are in the camp, "We should fight. We should go down fighting." After all, as a child

116

of the 1980s, she knows about fighting. She's probably seen *Rambo* two or three times. It's on cable TV. But Rifka laughs.

"What would we fight with?"

"With guns."

"We have no guns."

"With knives."

"Where are our knives?"

"With—with something."

Rifka put her arm around Hannah's shoulder. "Come. There is more work to be done."

"Work is not fighting."

"You want to be a hero, like Joshua at Jericho, like Samson against the Philistines." She smiled.

"I want to be a hero like…" Hannah thought a minute, came up with nothing.

"Who?"

"I don't know."

"My mother said before she…died…that it is much harder to live this way and to die this way than to go out shooting. Much harder. Chaya, you are a hero. I am a hero." Rifka stared for a moment at the sky and the curling smoke. "We are all heroes here."

What Hannah learns, what the child reader learns, is that history is full of heroes. We are all heroes here. Maybe not like King Arthur. Or Robin Hood. Or Joshua at Jericho. Or Rambo. We are small heroes. That is, after all, what history is really about—the small heroes. The ones who go across the mountains on faith and despite fear. The ones who get into a boat, believing the world is flat. The ones who gave their lives in the camps that others might live, and the ones who died in the camps just wanting to live another day.

We are all heroes here. Children need to know that was true back then and is true today. That it will be true tomorrow. It is a *living and continuous process* that they are part of.

The Devil's Arithmetic begins with the sentence "I'm tired of

remembering" and ends with the words "I remember, I remember."
Time travel books can give children back their memories by making
history an experiential act.

Throwing Shadows

Several years ago, my husband and I lived through a lifetime in ten days when we found ourselves in the middle of every parent's nightmare: the possibility of a beloved child dying.

To make a long and scary story short, all the tests came back negative, but we felt at the moment that a black line had been ruled through our lives, separating what we were before the possibility of the illness, and what we were afterwards.

I found myself really understanding for the first time that we humans live our lives through metaphor. Everything I felt during those dark days, the way I approached mortality, the way I prayed, the way I had to view the world, was in terms of metaphor. From the black line—which of course is not literal—to the dark days (we were actually in the middle of a light blush of Indian summer), to my ideas about death, to my instant-replay memories of the child who had twenty-six years earlier been in my womb, to my conversations and prayers and meditations and bargains with God. All were made up of metaphor.

So slowly, agonizingly, I came to understand that metaphor and her sisters—poetry and story—are as natural to humans as breathing. And further, I began to understand Archibald MacLeish's beautiful line in *Hypocrite Auteur*, "A world ends when its metaphor has died."

Then why are we mistrustful of metaphor?

Why do proponents of book banning cavil at stories with a fantastic, metaphoric presence?

Why do those of us who love stories with layers of meaning have to defend our interest, as if that very interest makes us less capable citizens, wimps, nerds, or in league with the very devil? (Which, of course, is in itself a metaphor.)

And why are children routinely taught metaphor as a part of grammar but not as a part of real life?

* * *

The idea that metaphor is important to human thinking is not new. It was old when Aristotle said, "To make metaphors implies an eye for resemblances." And, I suppose, one might add it implies an eye for differences as well.

To make a good metaphor, a writer has to be a good observer first, which—in some senses—is the measure of an educated person, whether that education took place in a school room, the workroom, the trenches, or the great outdoors. In Philip Wheelwright's telling phrase, "metaphor is a medium of fuller, riper knowing."

The world, too, has been going through its own dark days: Kosovo and the Serbian ethnic cleansing, devastation in Somalia, massacres in Africa, the murder of children by children in places like Littleton, and so on and on and on. These make my own personal ten days of terror nothing in comparison.

But what do we turn to when we have nothing left?

We turn to metaphor.

Mark Van Doren once wrote, "Wit is the only wall between us and the dark." That is as trenchant a metaphor as one can get. I wrote a very short story—fifty words exactly, though the title doesn't count—as part of a literary challenge once, trying to get at that very same thing.

"Story ," the old man said,

looking beyond the cave to the dragon's tracks. "Story is our wall against the dark." He told the tale: The landing, the first death, the second. They heard the rush of wind, the terrible voice, a scream, then another. Beyond the wall the dragon waited but could not get in.

This is, of course, story as poem as metaphor. The dragon is kept at bay because of the power of what we storytellers do.

I think of all the mothers who cradle their dying babies and tell them about the bright world ahead, not knowing for certain what is coming, but knowing that certainly the stories that they tell, the metaphors they couch their language in, brings comfort to both the children and themselves. For me the only moving part in the movie *Titanic* was when the Irish mother comforts her children in their bed, and as the water rises, tells them stories of Tir nan og.

***

I remember one particular child named Ann Marie and a nurse who sent me the following letter:

Dear Jane:

I was working at a children's hospital as the main person coordinating the child activity program. My work was with patients who were children, gravely ill, having chemotherapy or in some other way needing real support. I often used play therapy techniques or puppets, but if the children were too sick, I would read to them.

Ann Marie was an eleven-year-old girl who had been admitted by a doctor who didn't usually work with us. She had been sick for quite a while but not diagnosed, so by the time her therapy started she had many tumors. As the therapy started to kill the tumors, her kidneys and the cardiac system were also affected, so she had to be transferred to the ICU.

It appeared that she had always been an isolated and protected child, and the nurses referred to her as "young for her age."

The day I was to see her I was apprehensive. The times I had been in before she had been so sick, so filled with IVs and tubes and monitors, it was hard to think about the person inside that ailing repository of technology. So I picked at random a couple of books from the shelf and I went down to the ICU.

At first all I could think of was how sick she was. Her eyes were half open, her skin was yellow. She hardly moved except to turn her eyes toward me when I came in. I was in gown and mask as were all three nurses in there. They were just finishing her peritoneal dialysis and were preparing to leave.

I asked her what she would like me to read and she didn't answer. "Should I choose?" I asked. She nodded. And then I began reading your *Girl Who Loved the Wind* and the whole scene changed. The humming and beeping machines receded, the fear and pain stepped back into the corners of the room.

And I read this child a story that was all about her life and leaving. . .

When I finished reading the story, the two of us just sat together quietly. Two days later, she was dead. Her father and the doctors were shocked because it seemed so sudden, not expected.

But I know that the story truly served to comfort the departure of that child. In the morning after her death, after we had all cried and talked and wept about it, a beautiful stellar jay flew into our patio and came up and sat on the arm of the chair and looked into the bedroom at me where I lay still in bed. He sat there for almost a minute and I was filled then with a sense of peace. He seemed to say, "I come from Ann Marie and she's alright now."

My story had not been written with Ann Marie in mind, of course. But there was something in its central metaphor—about traveling beyond the known realms, about finding the courage to leave the past—that became a core metaphor for her. It helped her go somewhere with courage.

It was Ann Marie's wall against the dark.

Metaphor does that. It helps us explain ourselves to ourselves. It helps us explore and examine forces that we cannot otherwise come to terms with. We may call those forces God or Allah or Thor or

Coyote or Old Man or the White Goddess or any one of a billion other names. But they are all the same—they are the unknown that surrounds us.

A metaphor may indeed be an "exactly felt error," as John Ciardi has written. But we are the ones who feel it and, by holding tightly, take with us some small comfort into the dark.

Books for Further Reading

The essays in this book come from over thirty years of reading and writing about fantasy, faerie, and folklore in the literature of childhood. Over those years, a certain number of books and articles have remained as very special, helpful, stimulating companions and resources. I offer them here for those who want to read further.

How Basic Is Shazam?

Bettelheim, Bruno. *The Uses of Enchantment: The Meaning and Importance of Fairy Tales.* New York: A. A. Knopf, 1976.

Campbell, Joseph. *The Masks of God* (four volumes: *Primitive Mythology, Oriental Mythology, Occidental Mythology, Creative Mythology*). New York: Viking Press, 1959, 1969.

Dinesen, Isak. *Daguerreotypes and Other Essays.* Chicago: University of Chicago Press, 1979.

Duffy, Maureen. *The Erotic World of Faery.* London: Hodder & Staughton, 1972.

Migel, Parmenia. *Titania, the Biography of Isak Dinesen.* New York: Random House, 1967.

Yeats, W. B. *Irish Fairy and Folk Tales* (Introduction). New York: Modern Library, n.d.

The Lively Fossil

Andersen, Hans Christian. *The Complete Fairy Tales and Stories*, translated by Erik Christian Haugaard. New York: Doubleday, 1974.

Child, F. J. *English and Scottish Popular Ballads*, 5 vols. Boston: 1882–1898. (Dover has a complete reprint.)

Cox, Marian Roalfe. *Cinderella: 349 Variants*. London: David Nutt, 1893.

Opie, Iona and Peter. *The Classic Fairy Tales*. London: Oxford University Press, 1974.

Once Upon a Time

Auden, W. H. *The Dyer's Hand*. New York: Random House, 1962.

Cook, Elizabeth. *The Ordinary and the Fabulous*. Cambridge: Cambridge University Press, 1969.

Cox, Marian Roalfe. *Cinderella: 349 Variants*. London: David Nutt, 1893.

Jacobs, Joseph. *European Folk and Fairy Tales*. New York: G. P. Putnam's, 1916.

Opie, Iona and Peter. *The Classic Fairy Tales*. London: Oxford University Press, 1974.

Sale, Roger. *Fairy Tales and After*. Cambridge: Harvard University Press, 1978.

Schickel, Richard. *The Disney Version*. New York: Simon and Schuster, 1968.

Tolkien, J. R. R. "Children and Fairy Stories," *Only Connect*, edited by Egoff, Stubbs, and Ashley. Oxford: Oxford University Press, 1980.

The Eye and the Ear

Bettelheim, Bruno. *The Uses of Enchantment: The Meaning and Importance of Fairy Tales*. New York: A. A. Knopf, 1976.

Heins, Paul. *Snow White*. Boston: Atlantic Monthly Press, Little, 1974.

Jarrell, Randall. *Snow White*. New York: Farrar, Straus & Giroux, 1972.

Moray, Ann. *A Fair Stream of Silver*. New York: Morrow, 1965. (All about the Irish poets within society.)

Schaefer, Jack. *"If Stories Must Be Taught," Teaching Literature to Adolescents: Short Stories*, edited by Stephen Dunning. Chicago: Scott, Foresman, 1968.

Schickel, Richard. *The Disney Version*, New York: Simon and Schuster, 1968.

Touch Magic

Grahame, Kenneth. "Introduction," *A Hundred Fables of Aesop*. n. d.

Le Guin, Ursula. *The Language of the Night*. New York: G. P. Putnam's, 1979.

The Mask on the Lapel

Cameron, Eleanor. *The Green and Burning Tree.* Boston: Atlantic–Little, Brown, 1969.

Le Guin, Ursula. *The Language of the Night.* New York: G. P. Putnam's, 1979.

Tough Magic

Le Guin, Ursula. *The Language of the Night.* New York: G. P. Putnam's, 1979.

Opie, Iona and Peter. *The Classic Fairy Tales.* London: Oxford University Press, 1974.

Tolkien, J. R. R. "Children and Fairy Stories," *Only Connect,* edited by Egoff, Stubbs, and Ashley. Oxford: Oxford University Press, 1980.

Here There Be Dragons

Alexander, Lloyd. "The Flat-Heeled Muse," *Only Connect,* edited by Egoff, Stubbs, and Ashley. Oxford: Oxford University Press, 1980.

Lewis, C. S. "On Three Ways of Writing For Children," *Only Connect,* edited by Egoff, Stubbs, and Ashley. Oxford: Oxford University Press, 1980.

The Gift of Tongues

Eisler, Robert. *Man into Wolf: An Anthropological Interpretation of Sadism, Masochism, and Lycanthropy.* Santa Barbara, CA: Ross-Erickson, Inc., 1978.

Lane, Harlan. *The Wild Boy of Aveyron.* Cambridge: Harvard University Press, 1976.

MacLean, Charles. *The Wolf Children.* New York: Hill and Wang, 1977.

Singh J. A. L. and Robert M. Zingg. *Wolf Children and Feral Man.* New York: Harper & Brothers, 1942.

An Inlet for Apple Pie

Ciardi, John. "Everyone Wants To Be Published, But..." *The Writer Magazine,* August 1976.

Opie, Iona and Peter. The *Classic Fairy Tales.* London: Oxford University Press, 1974.

Story in Ten Fits

Nesbit, Edith. *The Phoenix and the Carpet.* New York: Viking, 1996.

Grahame, Kenneth. *The Wind in the Willows.* New York: Airmont, 1966.

Thurber, James. *The Thirteen Clocks.* New York: Simon & Schuster, 1950.

Egoff, Stubbs, and Ashley, ed. *Only Connect.* 3rd ed. Oxford: Oxford University Press, 1980.

Touchstones

Potter, Beatrix. *The Tale of Peter Rabbit.* St. Mineda, NY: Dover, 1972.

MacDonald, George. *The Golden Key.* Grand Rapids, MI: Eerdmans, 1980.

Kipling, Rudyard. *The Jungle Books.* New York: Airmont, 1966.

Thurber. *The Thirteen Clocks.* New York: Simon & Schuster, 1950.

White, E.B. *Charlotte's Web.* New York: HarperCollins, 1952.

Cameron, Eleanor. *The Green and Burning Tree.* Boston: Atlantic–Little, Brown, 1969.

Townsend, John Rowe. *Written for Children.* New York: J.B. Lippincott, 1983.

Fabling to the Near Night

Kingsley, Charles. *The Water Babies.* New York: Puffin, 1986.

Travers, Pamela L. *Mary Poppins.* New York: Buccaneer, 1981.

Dahl, Roald. *Charlie and the Chocolate Factory.* New York: Knopf, 1964.

Frye, Northrup. *The Anatomy of Criticism.* New York: Atheneum, 1966.

Zipes, Jack D. *Fairy Tales and the Art of Subversion.* New York: Routledge, 1985.

Broderick, Dorothy M. *Image of the Black in Children's Fiction.* New York: R.R. Bowker Company, 1973.

Killing the Other

Cashdan, Sheldon. *The Witch Must Die.* New York: Basic Books, 1999.

Opie, Iona and Peter. *The Classic Fairy Tales.* London: Oxford University Press, 1974.

An Experiential Act

Mayne, William. *Earthfasts.* New York: Peter Smith, 1990.

Pearce, Philippa. *Tom's Midnight Garden.* New York: HarperCollins, 1992.

Bond, Nancy. *A String in the Harp.* New York: Simon & Schuster, 1976.

Wells, H.G. *The Time Machine.* New York: Airmont, 1964.

Beckman, Thea. *Crusade in Jeans.* New York: Scribner & Sons, 1975.

Yolen, Jane. *The Devil's Arithmetic.* New York: Viking, 1988.

Kipling, Rudyard. *Puck of Pook's Hill.* New York: Amereon, Ltd., 1976.